A Spell of Spying

As she brought the bucket around to the back of the house to dump the wine-clouded water, Nola found her footsteps getting heavier and slower, until she stopped altogether. She'd recognized from the smell that that wine Kirwyn had spilled had been blackberry wine, and that put her in the mind once again of the man from Low Beck, the farmer who had hired them to pick blackberries. She remembered the strand of hair she had taken so long ago that morning. And she remembered that he had called her and her mother witches.

There was no reason to check to make sure the man wasn't plotting against them.

But she couldn't help herself.

Instead of taking the bucket back to the storage closet, she brought it down to the root cellar. Carefully she set the bucket on the floor. Very quietly she said the words that made the water receptive to shadowforms. With one last glance around to make sure she was alone, she tossed the hair of the blackberry farmer into the water.

The hair puckered the surface of the water, then shapes began to swirl and dance. They settled into the images of the man at his own kitchen table . . .

Other books by Vivian Vande Velde

Remembering Raquel
All Hallows' Eve: 13 Stories
Three Good Deeds
The Book of Mordred
Now You See It . . .
Wizard at Work
Heir Apparent
Being Dead
Alison, Who Went Away
The Rumpelstiltskin Problem
There's a Dead Person Following My Sister Around
Never Trust a Dead Man
A Coming Evil
Smart Dog
Curses, Inc., and Other Stories
Tales from the Brothers Grimm and the Sisters Weird
Companions of the Night
Dragon's Bait
User Unfriendly
A Well-Timed Enchantment
A Hidden Magic

For information about permission to reproduce selections from this book,
write to Permissions Department, Houghton Mifflin Harcourt Publishing
Company, 6277 Sea Harbor Drive, Orlando, Florida 32887-6777.

Graphia and the Graphia logo are registered trademarks of Houghton Mifflin Harcourt Publishing Company.

www.hmhbooks.com

The text of this book is set in Adobe Garamond.

The Library of Congress has cataloged the hardcover edition as follows:
Vande Velde, Vivian.
Magic can be murder/Vivian Vande Velde.
p. cm.
Summary: Nola and her mother have unusual abilities that have always
set them apart from others, but when Nola sees a murder using her
power to call up images using water and a person's hair, she finds herself
in the worst danger ever.
[1. Witchcraft—Fiction. 2. Murder—Fiction.] I. Title.
PZ7.V2773Mag 2000
[Fic]—dc2100-8595
ISBN: 978-0-15-202665-3
ISBN: 978-0-547-25872-0 pb

Manufactured in the United States of America
DOM 10 9 8 7 6 5 4 3 2 1

magic can be murder

VIVIAN VANDE VELDE

HOUGHTON MIFFLIN HARCOURT
BOSTON NEW YORK

magic can be murder

✷ PROLOGUE

THE FIRST TIME Nola and her mother fled a village to avoid being condemned as witches, Nola was five years old. Before that, Nola hadn't even realized she was a witch. She'd assumed everybody's mothers heard voices, and had never suspected there were people who couldn't change appearances—their own and others'—simply by wishing. She thought her mother didn't want her to read shadowforms in front of other people because Nola was so good at it—she already could call forth brighter and clearer images than her mother—and Nola thought her mother didn't want her showing off and making other people who maybe weren't so good at it feel bad.

But it's not showing off if you're just playing with your best friend, Nola reasoned.

So it began.

One afternoon in early spring when it was too cold and rainy to do anything outdoors, Nola and her best friend, Jane, ran out of everything they could agree on for indoors. They found themselves bored and only one step away from bickering. Nola's mother, along with the majority of Jane's family, was out planting in the fields, despite the damp. Nola and Jane were judged too young and more likely to get underfoot than to be of help, so they'd been left at the house of Jane's family, under the care of Jane's older sister, Bav. But Bav had left, an eternity ago it seemed, saying she had a short errand to run; and now there was nothing to do, nobody to tease or torment besides each other, and Jane whined—for the fourth or fifth time—"Where *is* she?"

"Well," Nola said, "why don't we go look in a bucket of water?"

"What would Bav be doing in a bucket of water?" Jane asked. She was laughing, so Nola thought she was joking.

"You get the water," Nola told her. "I'll find a hair on the pillow."

Bav's hair was darker and longer than any of her sisters', so Nola was able to tell which were hers in the bed the girls all shared. Back in the kitchen, Jane had set a bucket on the floor and was kneeling before it, peering inside.

"What are you doing?" Nola asked.

"Looking for Bav," Jane answered, once again laughing, her voice muffled from inside the bucket.

"Have you said the words and used a hair?"

Jane pulled her head out of the bucket. "What?"

Nola held up the strand of Bav's hair. "Have you said the words?"

Jane hesitated, looking—for some reason—confused. Then she shook her head.

Nola knelt beside her. Despite her silliness, Jane *had* put some water in the bucket, so now Nola said the words. They were in a language she didn't understand; she only knew they were the words for preparing water for shadowforms, just as there was another set of words for changing her own appearance, and yet another for changing how someone else looked. She would ask later, she thought, whether Jane knew where the words came from and what they meant. But for now, Nola said the words and, once the water was bespelled, dropped the strand of Bav's hair into the bucket.

She heard Jane's gasp of surprise, and assumed it was for the clarity of the shapes that formed and danced in the water. For a moment Jane even started to edge away from the soft glow as though alarmed, but then her curiosity drew her back. Apparently Bav's errand involved the woodwright's apprentice, for the images in the bucket showed the two of them in the barn. But this couldn't have been any errand her parents would have approved of; Nola saw that Bav and the apprentice were hugging and kissing and, judging by the straw in their hair and clothes, had been at it quite a while.

"Oooo," Jane said in delighted awe, "my father will beat the two of them silly." She shifted to get from kneeling to sitting, preparing for a good long watching,

3

and accidentally knocked her knee against the bucket's handle.

Nola lunged forward, but she overreached, so that her hand smacked against the bucket, sending it tipping and skittering across the floor.

The images of Bav and the woodwright's apprentice spread across the floor, oddly elongated and distorted before the dirt floor sucked up all the water and took the kissing lovers with it, leaving only a glistening spot of mud behind.

Jane righted the bucket, but there was only a wet smear on the bottom, not enough for shadowforms to dance. Still, she picked the strand of hair out of the mud and tossed it back in. As though that would cause anything to happen.

"It only works once," Nola said. Hadn't Jane's mother taught her anything? "If you want to do it again, we'll have to get another strand of hair and more water."

"All right," Jane said.

But this time Jane went to get the hair while Nola refilled the bucket. When Jane came back, she was holding a strand of white hair that obviously did not belong on Bav's dark head.

"Is this your mother's?" Nola asked as Jane settled down beside her, careful not to spill the newly refilled bucket. "All she's doing is planting—that's not so interesting to watch."

"It's my grandmother's," Jane said. "I found it on the shawl she used to wear."

Jane's grandmother had died during the coldest part of the past winter.

Jane asked, "Will we see her in heaven?"

Nola paused to consider. Shadowforms danced to whatever the owner of the hair was doing at the moment you were looking, so it seemed Jane had to be right: They'd see her grandmother in heaven. The only reason Nola hesitated was that she had never before called up the spell to see someone who had died, and—as far as she knew—her mother never had, either. Not even for Nola's father.

But maybe, Nola told herself, her mother had simply run out of her father's hairs—since each one could be used only once and he had died so long ago. So she said, "I don't know. Let's see. Do you want to say the words this time?"

Jane shook her head, so Nola once more said the spell. Then Jane dropped the white hair into the bucket.

The water quivered.

"It's too dark," Jane complained.

Nola concentrated. There *was* something, but she couldn't tell what.

"You're doing it wrong." Jane pouted, but she didn't offer to do it herself. After a long while, she began to sniffle. "She's not in heaven," she said, and the words, though barely whispered, released a storm of tears. "This can't be heaven."

She was right, Nola knew. It couldn't be. She threw her arm around her friend, to comfort her, and shifted her eyes away from the vague still form in the water. She looked, instead, at the dirt floor on which the bucket sat. And there she found the answer.

Dirt. That was what they were looking at. "It's her grave," Nola said. "We're seeing inside her grave."

That realization left no question about the dark shape looming in the corner, which resolved itself into a rotting shroud, with bits of hair showing through. Instead of being comforted, Jane began to cry even louder.

Such a fuss, Nola thought—though she understood she might feel differently if it were her own grandmother. "That doesn't mean she isn't in heaven," she said. "It just means her body is buried. The shadowforms are showing us what her body is doing, and her body is lying in the ground."

But Jane just shoved her away.

And that was when the door opened, and Nola's mother and Jane's mother both walked in.

They had obviously come to complain that Bav had not yet delivered the midday meal, but as soon as Jane's mother saw her daughter's tears, her expression went from annoyed to alarmed. "What's happened?" She glanced around the room. "Where's Bav? Are you hurt?"

Nola's mother was frightened, too—Nola could tell by her eyes. She grabbed Nola by the arm and dragged her to her feet, at the same time kicking over the bucket, sending strand of hair and water and shadowforms spilling across the kitchen floor. "What are you doing?" she demanded.

But before Nola could get out more than, "I—," her mother smacked her on the side of the head so hard that her ears rang.

"What foolish game are you playing to frighten your little friend?" her mother demanded, which made no sense at all because her mother was the one who had taught her how to bespell water. Her mother knew it wasn't a foolish game. But her mother shook her head and said—though Jane's mother was kneeling on the floor and rocking Jane and obviously not listening— "The girl *will* defy me. It comes of having no father." And she grabbed Nola by her still-stinging ear and dragged her out the door and into the dripping afternoon. Behind them, they could hear Jane crying, gulping, occasionally managing to whimper, "Grandmother..."

"What did you do?" Nola's mother asked in a fierce whisper, shaking Nola. "Haven't I told you never, never, never to talk about witchcraft in front of other people? And now you actually perform a spell?"

Witchcraft? Bespelling water was witchcraft? Nola hadn't known. But she remembered seeing an old woman driven out of the village, people hurling stones at her back, for being a witch. And Nola knew she didn't want that to happen to her or her mother. So she told exactly what she had done.

Her mother said, "Start walking," and they didn't

even tarry long enough to go to their own house next door for a change of clothes.

That was the first time.

❦

YEARS PASSED. Nola learned that she could not hold on to friends, but that she and her mother had to keep moving, wandering from village to village lest anyone start pointing at them for imagined wrongs or a string of bad luck.

Nola also learned that if she was caught referring to something that she had learned by looking into water, she must admit to the lesser evil: that she was a busybody, listening where she shouldn't have been. Eventually she looked in water to see what other people were doing only if she desperately *needed* to know whether someone was beginning to suspect her.

But that was the only magic she worked. She never, ever, changed her appearance, because it was exhausting work to keep a magically created form, and glamours always disappeared when the caster fell asleep. She couldn't risk being found out.

With all Nola learned, life should have gotten easier. But over the years, Nola's mother began to make less and less sense. For Nola's mother heard voices inside her head, and as time passed the voices became louder, and more varied, and more argumentative. "Quiet!" she would yell—among the market stalls, or by the stream where the village women washed their clothes, or in the kitchens where Nola and her mother sometimes found work—it made no difference where. "I can make my own decisions!" she would shout, or, "One at a time! How can I concentrate if all of you chatter at once?"

When Nola had been young, she had assumed the voices were real: ghosts or spirits that, if unruly, still were there to guide her mother, to let her know the future, or to give her knowledge.

But as Nola got older, she saw that the voices tormented her mother and offered useless or conflicting advice. Some voices seemed to belong to people who had died—Nola's father, Nola's mother's own mother. But there was also someone her mother called King Fenuku the Flatulent—a name Nola was fairly certain had never been given to the ruler of any land—not to mention an unborn baby her mother was convinced lived in her left forefinger.

So it was that the suspicion of witchcraft always fell on the mad mother rather than on the quiet daughter.

Despite all this, their lives, though unsettled, were still patterned and somewhat predictable: the search for work, the search for food and shelter, the passing friendships—quickly made and quickly broken.

But, of course, Nola knew that could last only so long.

✪ CHAPTER ONE

THE MORNING HAD started with promise.

Her mother was having one of her more rational days. "Your father," she told Nola as the two of them worked side by side picking blackberries for a man whose wife considered herself too fine for field work, "was a kind and gentle man."

When her father had died, Nola had been little more than a baby, so that now, at seventeen, she couldn't remember his face. But she'd been old enough to remember that he *had* been kind and gentle.

"He was," she said with a smile, recalling rides given on strong, broad shoulders, and tickling that never went on too long.

Nola straightened, trying to work the kink out of her back quickly, before the man who had hired them noticed and came over to complain. He was obviously suspicious of something, because every time Nola glanced in his direction, he was watching her.

"But your father," Nola's mother continued in that

same reasonable voice, "doesn't like the way that man is looking at you. Your father suggests I go over there and kick him hard in the kneecap. Oh-oh. Too late. That man's heading over here now."

So much for rational days.

"Mother!" Nola protested. She bent down quickly, hoping to deflect the man by showing evidence of hard work.

"Don't blame me," Nola's mother protested. "It's your father who said it, not me. 'Kick and run,' he said. 'That's no way for someone to be looking at MY daughter.'"

"I don't care who said it," Nola whispered between her teeth. "Don't you dare *do* it." The sun was beating hot on her head and shoulders, so that sweat ran, tickling her scalp and stinging her eyes. *Of course that man's looking at me THAT WAY,* she told herself. *Doesn't everyone find sweat and dirt and stink appealing? It's amazing he's resisted this long.*

But her mother was right about one thing: He was approaching. Nola heard the rustle as he moved through the bushes, and then his shadow fell over her, a moment of coolness on her bare arms. She didn't look up, but continued picking berries and tossing them into the basket beside her. Was he going to complain that she was picking too slowly and not doing enough work? Or that she was picking too quickly and bruising the fruit?

"You look hot," he said, not sounding annoyed after all. "Would you like some fresh water?"

She finally did look up, from his knobby knees to his face, which—if not handsome—at least was not ugly; and from his face she moved her gaze to his hand, which was holding a glazed pot with lovely droplets of water running glistening down its surface. She looked back to his face and this time found it not only not ugly, but kind.

"Oh, many thanks," she told him. The bucket of water she and her mother were sharing had grown warm in the sun. Even at the beginning the water had tasted of old wood, and as the morning progressed it had picked up the additional tang of dirt and sweat.

The jug felt cool in her hands, though she was aware that her fingers left muddy streaks on the damp surface where she grasped it. She wiped her hand on her skirt, but that hardly helped. On the outside of the jug, where the handle was attached, a single strand of hair was held captive by the dampness.

Nola collected hairs. She couldn't help herself, couldn't let them pass. There was no telling when she might need one. With a gesture too small to alert the unsuspecting, Nola caught up the hair—short and black, it belonged to the man, not his wife—and wrapped it around her fingertip.

With a glance at her mother that warned, *Don't say anything,* she took a long, satisfying gulp of the cool water. She handed the jug to her mother, who—thankfully—said nothing.

"Thank you," Nola repeated, making to hand the jug

back to the man after her mother had had her fill. She assumed he would make his way down the path to where his brother's wife and children also picked berries.

But, "Finish it," the man said, smiling. "It's lighter empty than full."

He must mean to go back to the well to get another jugful for his brother's family, she reasoned. But at the same time, the thought tickled at her mind that he had come to her and her mother first, rather than to his kinfolk.

"Cool yourself down," he suggested. "Pour it over your shoulders." But though he said *shoulders,* it wasn't her shoulders he was staring at.

At which point Nola decided that regardless of who had originally said it—her mother or her father—she also did not like the way this man was looking at her.

"Not necessary," she told him, and once more tried to hand the jug back.

"It's something I've seen the women in the fields do," he told her. "They pour water on their hands then run their hands…" He indicated an area of bare skin definitely below shoulder level.

"Ah!" Nola said. "No doubt a trick you learned from your wife." She had seen the wife, who had been the one to answer the door when Nola and her mother had knocked, seeking work: a common woman, Nola had judged from their few moments' acquaintance, who put on airs.

Now the woman's husband grinned and shrugged. "And from my sister-in-law," he said, though obviously he wasn't interested in whether his sister-in-law stayed cool or overheated today. "And others. Why don't you come over to the shade of the peach tree? Lie down. Rest." His voice was calm and rational, and there was no reason to suspect he meant more than he said, except... Except that Nola did.

The man continued, "The tree can't be seen from the house. My wife is a hard woman who would work you to death. She never needs to know." He ran his tongue over the lip of the jug at the spot from where Nola had drunk.

"Please," Nola said. If she left now, all the work that she and her mother had done the whole morning long would be for nothing.

The man looked at her quizzically, as though to say he had no idea what she was asking.

"I don't want any trouble," Nola said. She could try making a complaint to the town magistrate, but how likely was he to believe her? She imagined her voice, high-pitched and nervous, explaining, *Nobody here knows me or my mother, but we worked for the majority of the morning for this man, and then we had to leave without payment because he wouldn't let me be.* Maybe the sister-in-law—if he had paid unwanted attention to her—would back her story with experience of her own. But maybe the attention wasn't unwanted in the sister-in-law's case, or maybe she had too much to lose by making a complaint against her kinsman.

Nola thought of the state of her hair and clothes. She

could imagine the magistrate saying, *This man is a respected member of our community, and you...*

Why even try to work out what the magistrate would say? She and her mother would never seek him out. They couldn't afford the attention.

The man took hold of her arm, not roughly, sure she wouldn't resist. "Come," he said.

"You know," Nola said, to give her mother warning, though her mother seemed elsewhere, elsewhen, standing there swaying slightly, humming a lullaby to herself. "You know, my father once gave me some good advice..."

She kicked the man's knee and ran. The man dropped the water jug, which shattered when it hit the ground. She could hear him yelping and cursing behind her, but louder, closer, she could hear her mother, cackling and laughing, as she ran also, keeping up as Nola ran out from between the bushes, cut across the corner of a fallow field, and leaped over a short stone fence onto the road.

"Your father says to tell you, 'Well done!'" her mother said. Then she turned back and shouted to the man in the blackberry field, "And King Fenuku says to tell *you*..." She hoisted up her skirt and pointed her rear end in his direction.

"You crazy old witch!" the man yelled, which turned Nola's blood to ice water, even though he showed no inclination to follow. "You're both crazy witches!" He must have realized then that he would have to find an excuse to give his wife. "And you owe me for that jug you broke!"

"Turn him into a toad, Nola!" her mother crowed. "Turn him into a toad!"

"Mother!" Nola cried, hoping they were too far away for the man to have heard.

Her mother got her disappointed, sulky expression. "He'd only *look* like a toad," she muttered in complaint. "He wouldn't really *be* one." As though that wouldn't count. "And it would only last a day."

"Enough," Nola warned. A five-foot-tall toad. How likely was *that* to go unnoticed?

The day couldn't get any worse, Nola thought as she started walking.

But of course it could.

✿ CHAPTER TWO

WALKING FROM NOON till evening, Nola and her mother ended up in a town called Haymarket. It seemed a prosperous place, but apparently every homeowner and business had just enough help to keep things running smoothly. As night closed in around them, Nola began to think they might end the day with no supper. No shelter, either.

"We'll ask as far as the end of this street," Nola told her mother, which meant three more houses. "If we don't find something here..." She was too weary to finish and just waved vaguely toward the setting sun. They'd seen a barn earlier. The fact that the barn looked ready to fall down didn't mean its owners would be willing to let them stay there, so it was best to go after nightfall and not bother to ask permission.

"Good," her mother said. She was cradling her left arm, humming a lullaby to her finger. "The baby is getting tired."

"Just..." Nola didn't know how to finish the thought

Don't let the baby cry? Don't say anything about the baby where people can hear? Don't do anything to ruin whatever small chance we have?

She knocked on the door. *Probably not loud enough,* she realized. Most likely she'd need to summon the energy to knock again.

But a young woman of seventeen or eighteen opened the door. She might have been the same age as Nola— but she had the look of someone who could take things for granted from day to day: things like that she would most probably eat that day, and the next, and that she would sleep with a roof overhead, and that her mother probably wouldn't get the two of them run out of town or killed for being witches.

"I…," Nola started. But she'd lost track of what it was she had been going to say.

The young woman at the door supplied the words for her. "You're looking for work?"

Or a meal. Or a corner to sleep in—warmth and dryness welcome, but not expected.

Nola nodded her head. But then—since she knew what the answer would be—she turned to leave.

"Wait here," the woman told her. "This is exceptional good luck."

It is? Nola thought.

"Kirwyn," the young woman called into the kitchen behind her. "Master Kirwyn."

But Kirwyn, whoever he was, wasn't there.

"Wait here," the woman repeated as though afraid

Nola would wander off into the evening gloom. She didn't even close the door behind her to make Nola wait outside, as though it never occurred to her that a stranger presented with an open house might run in and steal something.

Nola rested her head on the doorjamb and may or may not have drifted into a few moments' sleep as she stood there. She jerked her head up at the sound of a male voice, loud, but from another room, that demanded, "What in the world do we need more people in the house for now?"

Ah, well, Nola thought. So much for exceptional good luck. But the woman had told her to stay, so Nola stayed. Behind her, her mother was swaying gently, still humming.

Whatever the woman answered—Nola presumed she answered something, because she didn't come right back out again—whatever she answered, Nola couldn't hear her. Once again, Nola dozed on her feet. The sound of approaching footsteps roused her.

The woman came back with two men. One was a sulky-faced youth—Nola immediately connected him with the whining voice that had wanted to send her away—and the other was an older man, with enough family resemblance to the first that Nola concluded they must be father and son.

"This is Master Innis," the woman said, "whose work as a silversmith is so fine that he has customers from as far away as Linchester."

Servant, Nola thought, from the woman's tone. She hadn't been sure before. Wife or daughter-in-law might sound proud, but not so self-consciously flattering.

"And who have we here?" the silversmith asked.

Nola curtsied. "I am Nola. And this is my mother—"

"Mary," Nola's mother interrupted—which was not her name, but at least it was a more seemly name than Eurydice, which she had used in Low Beck, the last town.

Master Innis looked impatient, and Nola realized he hadn't really been interested in their names. The son continued to look sour.

Nola curtsied again. "We are seeking work."

No doubt he had already been told that to get him out here. The silversmith looked at Nola and her mother appraisingly. "Overly thin," he mused, as someone might comment on a horse or hound.

"But strong," Nola assured him. "And willing to work hard."

Something else one might say about horse or hound.

He was looking over her shoulder. Nola was determined not to turn. Best not to know what her mother was doing, since there was no way to stop her, nor to keep anyone from noticing, if she *was* doing something embarrassing or likely to get them into trouble.

Her resolve didn't last. She couldn't help herself. She made as though to knead a tired shoulder, and shot a glance backward, but her mother wasn't doing anything.

Or—at least—she wasn't doing anything anymore.

Turning back to the silversmith, Nola gave as bright a smile as she could manage.

"Well," Innis said, not sounding quite convinced, "Brinna needs the help, for I will be married within the week and this house needs to be cleaned and prepared for my new wife."

The young servant woman, Brinna, looked pleased with herself and the world now that there were two newer servants to help her.

The son, Kirwyn, wore the expression of one who was sure their upkeep would come straight from his own pocket.

"Congratulations," Nola's mother chirped to the about-to-be-married silversmith.

Nola opened her mouth to offer her best wishes also, but she didn't have a chance.

"Congratulations," Nola's mother repeated in a slightly different voice, brisk and efficient, the voice Nola recognized as the one her mother used when speaking on behalf of Mother Superior. And then a third time, in a lower tone, probably one of the men, "Congratulations."

Kirwyn scowled. Even Brinna's smile faded. Only Nola's did not. *Trust us,* her smile said. *We're harmless.*

"Yes," the silversmith said, more slowly now. "Well. Come in, then."

✿ CHAPTER THREE

Nola and her mother had come too late in the day to do any work and were in time only to eat, Kirwyn pointed out. Two or three times he pointed it out.

"Enough!" his father finally said. "Kirwyn, you whine and complain like an old fishwife without two pennies to rub together. They will have work enough tomorrow. And if after we have fed them they should run away without working, that will hardly cause our financial ruin."

Nola, who very rarely had two pennies herself, felt Master Innis was too harsh in his opinion of fishwives. She knew it hardly counted as work to prepare a meal she herself would eat, but she couldn't help resenting the way Kirwyn complained of her: If she wasn't getting much accomplished, it was because he kept getting in her way so that she had to walk around him while she carried in buckets of water from the well and as she readied the table.

Her mother, set in the corner to chop a few extra carrots and to peel an onion, periodically chuckled to herself, but not enough to draw more than passing glances.

Of course, Master Innis and Kirwyn were served first, and it was only when they were finished with their meal that the servants were allowed to sit and eat. The other servant, besides Brinna and now Nola and her mother, was a man named Alan, who was somewhere in age between Kirwyn and his father. Mostly he worked in the shop helping the silversmith, but apparently he did not consider himself above the household servants. Or at least not above Brinna, Nola thought, noting the way his eyes sparkled whenever he watched her. Kirwyn noted this also, Nola saw, when he came into the kitchen while they were cleaning up.

Except that nobody saw Kirwyn until it was too late.

Nola and Brinna were on their knees, scrubbing the stone floor of the kitchen. Nola's mother was trying hard to bring back a shine to a pot that hadn't shone in years. Alan, who'd put away the last of the dishes, approached Brinna from behind, then gave her a playful whack on the bottom.

"Alan!" Brinna protested. But she was laughing. She threw the wet cloth at his stomach, splattering sudsy water both on the man and on the just-cleaned table.

"Oh, good job, Brinna!" Alan laughed. He shook a warning finger at her and said, obviously imitating Kirwyn, "You must take your household duties more seriously!"

"So should you all," Kirwyn said from the doorway.

That was the first notice they had of his presence, and it wiped the smiles off their faces.

"Alan, go tell my father you have too much time on your hands and see you what he needs done. Do you think the shop runs itself? My father needs to concentrate on the making and fashioning of silver—not on whether there's enough wood for the fire or if the goods are polished to show them off to their best advantage."

Alan looked as if he was about to say something— probably that he had already laid in the next day's wood supply, or that the silversmith had already said enough for the day—but he bit off an answer that could only get him into trouble. He ducked his head and edged out of the room.

Next Kirwyn's attention alighted on Nola's mother. "You, old hag, fetch extra blankets from the storage closet for yourself and your daughter, and make up beds. Tomorrow morning will come soon enough, and if you don't make sleeping arrangements until bedtime, you will disrupt us all."

He turned on Nola. Over his shoulder, Nola saw her mother making the sign to avert the evil eye. Brinna, fortunately, took that as funny, and placed a hand over her mouth to cover a giggle. Nola, who was tired enough to go to sleep then and there, tried to look alert and interested, and most definitely not distracted by anything going on behind Kirwyn's back. Her mother set the still-blackened pot down and left the kitchen—one could only hope she was headed for the storage closet.

To Nola, Kirwyn said, "As for you, your work starts tonight rather than tomorrow morning. I spilled some wine in my room. My bedding needs to be changed and cleaned before the stains set."

"Yes, Master Kirwyn." Nola curtsied to hide the dismay on her face. She fervently hoped cleaning was all Kirwyn had on his mind.

But Kirwyn wasn't interested in her. She saw that a moment later as he tried to snake his arm around Brinna's waist.

"Master Kirwyn," Brinna protested, deftly dodging him. She'd retrieved the wet rag and she flipped it as she turned, so that it spattered—apparently all unintended—on Kirwyn.

A pretty girl like Brinna, Nola realized as she headed for Kirwyn's room, would have had practice enough avoiding unwanted attention. *She* wouldn't have caused a scene the way Nola had with the blackberry farmer in Low Beck. Of course, Nola could look pretty, too. She could cast a glamour spell and make herself lovely: stunning, exotic, breathtakingly gorgeous, the kind of woman men wrote poems for and sang ballads about. But what was the point? It was safer to look unremarkable, so people wouldn't notice her, wouldn't remember her, wouldn't bother her. Plain as she was, she'd had a close call today.

Working by the light of the candle she had brought with her, Nola stripped Kirwyn's bed. He had apparently tried to catch the goblet as it tipped off the nightstand

and had sent it flying even farther, spraying wine over the top of his clothes chest and onto the tapestry that covered the wall behind. She needed a bucket of water and a rag but didn't want to go back to the kitchen for fear of Kirwyn, so she went to the storage closet. She could hear her mother humming her lullaby in the room next door, the room they would be sharing with Brinna. From the sounds, her mother must have been stuffing the mattresses as she had been instructed.

There was, indeed, an extra bucket in the closet, and Nola got it, filled it with water, and brought it back to Kirwyn's room. Dabbing at the wine stain that had soaked into the mattress, she worked quickly, hoping to be done and gone before he came back. Then she flipped the mattress over, dry side up, and fetched fresh blankets from the clothes chest. She mopped up the wine from the rug by the bed and from the top of the chest, then she did the best she could with the tapestry. Tomorrow she would do a better job by taking the tapestry down, but if she did so tonight, Kirwyn was sure to complain of the cold draft off the wall.

As she brought the bucket around to the back of the house to dump the wine-clouded water, Nola found her footsteps getting heavier and slower, until she stopped altogether. She'd recognized from the smell that the wine Kirwyn had spilled had been blackberry wine, and that put her in mind once again of the man from Low Beck, the farmer who had hired them to pick blackberries. She remembered the strand of hair she had taken so long ago that morning. And she remembered, not only his unwanted advances, but that he had called them witches.

Had he really thought so, or was he only angry?

You're being foolish, she told herself. Surely other women—even other unremarkable women such as herself—had taken offense at his suggestions before. He couldn't suspect her of being a witch just because of that.

That, she reminded herself, and her mother's constant mumblings and oddities.

And the fact that he might have seen her take and save that strand of his hair.

But wouldn't he have said something *then* if he had noticed?

Unless he had assumed she was flirting with him by taking that hair.

Though surely her later actions disproved that.

Maybe—if he *had* seen her take the hair—he simply didn't know what to make of such an action.

And that meant she was safe.

Unless he mentioned it to someone else. Someone who knew the tricks of witches.

Don't wish troubles onto yourself, she tried to convince herself, *troubles that don't even exist. You're overtired and not thinking properly.*

There was no reason to suspect that the silversmith's household bought their blackberries from the man in Low Beck, and there was no reason to check to make sure the man wasn't plotting against them.

But she couldn't help herself.

Instead of taking the bucket back to the storage closet, she brought it down to the root cellar. That the water was wine colored and only as deep as the breadth of two or three fingers would not trouble the spell. Carefully she set the bucket on the floor. Very quietly she said the words that made the water receptive to shadowforms. Then she took from her bodice the little square of unbleached wool where she had placed the man's hair. She had another square of cloth in which she had collected two hairs off the comb on Kirwyn's nightstand and one from the cloak he had thrown over a chair. Not that she was interested in Kirwyn. But Nola always gathered strands of hair when she could, just in case she needed them later, as she needed the farmer's hair now. Nola congratulated herself on being clever. With one last glance around to make sure she was alone, she tossed the hair of the blackberry farmer into the water.

The hair puckered the surface of the water, then shapes began to swirl and dance. They settled into the image of the man at his own kitchen table. His wife was sitting across from him, mending a shirt by candlelight. The man was snoring. For long moments nothing changed, then the woman finished her sewing and very quietly—voices always just barely came through—she said, "Are you coming to bed or not?"

Nola saw her pick up the candle, and her husband scratched himself noisily and yawned as though to swallow the entire bucket of water that contained him. He stood; but as he stood, he winced, rubbing at the knee

Nola had kicked. His lips twitched soundlessly. It didn't take much to guess that what he muttered to himself was the word "witch." Then he followed his wife to bed and the two of them got in without exchanging another word. In another few moments, they were both snoring.

So much for him setting the town magistrate or witch-hunters onto her trail.

Nola put her hand on the edge of the bucket to overturn it, which would end the spell.

Except that the farmer was still sore and angry. What if he made his move tomorrow?

Only one hair. Only one spell. A spell she had wasted by doing it at bedtime.

Pouring the water out of the bucket would dispel the magic. But Nola wasn't willing to do that. Once that was done, the strand of hair she had slid off the surface of the jug would never again be able to summon forth shadowforms from water.

Nola couldn't be satisfied with this one picture of quiet in the home of the blackberry farmer. Instead of upending the bucket, she pushed it beneath the stairs. She draped her cleaning rag over it to hide it from sight, even though, she assured herself, no one was likely to come down here to the root cellar any time soon—not during summer, when there were fresh foods to be had. And even if someone did come, she told herself, even if someone came and saw the rag and picked it up off the bucket, even then they weren't likely to see the shadowshapes, if they weren't expecting to see them, not in this

29

dim light. And the voices were too little to carry, especially from under the cloth.

This way she could check on the farmer again tomorrow. If things were still quiet, she would end the spell then.

She went back to the kitchen to help Brinna clean up, but Brinna had finished already and gone to bed. Nola could hear Kirwyn and his father in another room of the house—not exactly arguing, she didn't think, but sounding as though they were disagreeing about something.

"Good night," Alan called to her from his cubbyhole by the stairs.

"Good night," Nola wished him back.

✿ CHAPTER FOUR

THE MORNING WAS full with the making of breakfast, the starting of soup for the noon meal, the baking of breads, the putting down of fresh rushes beneath the kitchen table—daily work that was done quickly with two extra sets of hands to help Brinna's. And then there was the beating of rugs and wall hangings, the laundering of all the linens and clothing in the household save what was currently being worn, the restuffing of Master Innis's mattress with sweet-smelling herbs—all in preparation for the arrival of the silversmith's new bride, Sulis, in five more days.

There was not an extra moment for Nola to slip away to see what the shadowforms in the bucket of water were doing.

But, of course, she made the time.

When she first managed to sneak into the root cellar, she saw that the blackberry farmer from Low Beck was still asleep in bed.

So she tried again.

The second time she managed to slip away, his entire attention was concentrated on mending a boot. Totally useless.

She was about to open the door to the cellar a third time—she already had her hand on the door—when she realized Brinna was watching her. Brinna had been standing at the end of the hall on Nola's previous visit, too.

You're going to bring suspicion and trouble upon yourself where otherwise there would be none, Nola chided herself.

The bucket was safe where it was. No one would go down there unless *she* led them there. And *if* someone did happen to go downstairs, the bucket was situated in a corner where it could not be easily seen. Anyway, who besides a witch would take the time to look into a bucket of water long enough to make out the shapes of living people within?

There would be time enough in the afternoon, or after supper, to see what the man with the blackberries was doing. Once more Nola told herself, *And what he will be doing will be nothing.* Angry as he might be for the unexpected rebuff, for the kick in the knee, how much explanation did he want to give his wife or the magistrate? Far better for him to say, "Those women were not only lazy, they were clumsy. So when they broke the jug that carried the water I had so thoughtfully left with them, they ran away rather than be held accountable for the replacing of it."

Still, all in all Nola craved reassurance, and she did

not regret setting up the spell and leaving it untended.

Not until it was time for the noonday meal did she regret it.

All morning Innis, his son, Kirwyn, and the servant Alan had been working in the wing of the dwelling that served as the silversmith's shop. Then Alan came into the kitchen to say the master was ready to eat and would have his meal in the shop. Brinna set the food on two trays—Alan carried one, Nola's mother the other—while Nola readied the kitchen table for the servants' meal.

She was just ladling out the last of the soup when she heard a crash from the other end of the house, followed by the sound of upraised voices. She abandoned the ladle in the pot and was faster even than Brinna in racing down the hall and into the shop.

One of the trays was on the floor, wooden bowl and bronze goblet overturned, with chunks of bread and cheese sitting like islands in the spreading sea of soup and wine mixing together. The brownish mess oozed around the leg of one of the display tables and over the jewelry and the belt buckles that lay in a heap on the stone floor, apparently knocked there by the falling tray.

Nola didn't have to wonder who had dropped the tray—whether it was her mother or Alan. She had known it was her mother even before she had seen that a tray had been dropped.

The remaining tray was set safely on one of the other tables, and Alan was just going down into a crouch, already using his hands to try to stop the flow of soup and wine from spreading over any more of the fallen silver trinkets.

Nola's mother, however, had backed against the wall, and she was holding her hands up to form a cross with her two forefingers. "Back, Death, back!" she was shouting over and over, though whether at Innis or Kirwyn wasn't clear.

"You crazy old fool!" Kirwyn shouted back at her, and the louder he got, the louder she became, so the louder he got....

"The necklace!" Innis yelled at Alan. "No, no, not the one that's already covered! Save the—" Innis threw his hands up and gave a growl of frustration as the puddle of wine-diluted soup seeped around Alan's hands and over an intricately worked piece of silver. Innis gestured for Alan to shove the remaining jewelry out of the spreading path of soup, but Alan's hands were brown and sticky and now surely it would all have to be cleaned anyway.

But Nola was not concerned with the jewelry. "Mother!" she called sharply.

Her voice didn't snap her mother out of whatever fit this was. "He's dead, dead, oh woe!" her mother said, almost in a chant now, her voice shrill and frightened. If she even recognized Nola, she gave no sign of it.

What new disaster was this? Nola's embarrassment and the slow, steady dread of discovery withered in the face of this unaccustomed behavior.

34

Nola had seen people slap someone who was hysterical, but she couldn't bring herself to strike her own mother. She had to fight harder to suppress the inclination to slap Kirwyn. He was continuing to berate them both—and Brinna as well for asking to hire them, and his father for agreeing.

"Mother!" Nola repeated more loudly, more firmly. Then, despite the danger that her panicked mother didn't know her and might lash out, Nola went up to her. She intentionally placed herself between her mother and the men, and put her arms around her mother, and hoped that the men would think...

What would be a good thing for them to think?

"It's all right, Mother," she said. "They won't beat you. They know it was an accident."

Could they be convinced that her mother was terrified of being beaten for clumsiness—that they had misunderstood what she had said?

"Death," her mother repeated, but not so frantically. Even more encouraging was that her mother appeared to know her.

"No one means to kill you," Nola said, and opened her mouth to weave a story about a time when an irate chatelaine had threatened—

But her mother destroyed any possibility of excuses by saying, "Death stands by him."

And Kirwyn, of course, picked that same moment to stop haranguing them, so that Nola's mother's words sounded loud and clear, like the clang of a leper's bell.

There was no chance of anyone misunderstanding that.

"What?" Kirwyn said. Then, even though Nola's mother had snaked her arm around Nola and was clearly pointing at Kirwyn's father, he asked, "Who?"

"You think you see Death standing by my side?" Innis asked, in a voice that was remarkably calm for the circumstances.

"Of course not!" Nola's mother snapped. "I don't have second sight, do I?"

"Then what—," Nola and at least two of the others in the room simultaneously started.

"*Abbot Dinsmore* has second sight," Nola's mother said, obviously exasperated with all of them. "Abbot Dinsmore started saying the Mass of the Dead. For him." Again her finger shook in Innis's direction.

Nola smacked her mother's hand away, hoping that she gave the appearance of only raising her own hand to reassuringly caress her mother's cheek. *Who in the world is Abbot Dinsmore?* she wondered. But even as she wondered she knew. She'd never heard the name before, but she knew. *Not a new voice, not now.* It was always worst when a new voice started: "They keep pushing and shoving for room," her mother would complain, smacking the side of her head. "Stop shouting in there—I can hear you perfectly well."

Now, still trying to save the situation by covering it over with a babble of words, Nola said innocently, "Abbot Dinsmore? You mean that poor demented pilgrim we met along the way, who mumbled away in Latin half the time, and…"—she partially turned to address Innis—"he thought he was a priest, though I doubt he ever was, and he was saying snatches of novenas and—"

"Nola!" her mother rebuked her. "We *never* met anyone like that. What gets into you?" And she sounded perfectly rational, except that she pointed to her head and said, "I'm talking about Abbot Dinsmore who lives in here with the rest of them, of course. And he gets glimpses into the future, and as soon as he saw the silversmith over there, he began to say the Mass of the Dead."

And how could anyone cover up a statement like that?

To Innis, Nola's mother said, "I'm *so* sorry to hear you're going to be dying soon."

"Perhaps," Innis said, only somewhat shakily, "it would be best if you left—both of you."

It was Alan who stood up for them. "She's just an old woman whose wits have begun to wander," he said.

Nola nodded vigorously. "She means no harm."

"I realize that," Innis said. "But practically on the eve of my wedding…" He shook his head. "It isn't lucky."

How could she begin to argue with that?

"But they've worked all morning." Now it was Brinna who protested. Brinna, who would once more be on her own to prepare the house for the new bride.

Innis said, "They may eat before they go."

Even Kirwyn, who had whined so of their hire, had a good word, of sorts. "How will Brinna ever manage on her own before Sulis arrives?"

"I have spoken," Innis announced.

And that was the end of that job.

✿

BESIDES GIVING them lunch, Brinna packed food for them to take. "I know what it is like to be hungry," she told them.

So Nola and her mother once again walked till nightfall, and when they stopped they were in the town of Saint Erim Turi, which was bigger than four or five of Haymarket.

Nola liked big towns. People of wealth who were disinclined to hard work often congregated in such places, and it was usually possible to find someone to take them in.

It was also easier, she comforted herself, to lose yourself and not have people notice you.

She began to relax, confident at last that they were far enough away and in a big enough town that no one would come tracking them down—not Innis, who in any case did not seem apt to, nor the blackberry farmer from Low Beck.

The blackberry farmer from Low Beck.

Standing in the middle of the street as they looked for a good place to spend the night, Nola thought for the first time of the bucket in the silversmith's root cellar, the bucket bespelled with a strand of the blackberry man's hair in it, and everything the blackberry man did acting out in the water there.

Oh no, she thought. *Oh no, oh no, oh no.*

"What?" her mother asked, for Nola had stopped so suddenly that her mother had to come back to fetch her.

"Nothing," Nola managed to breathe out.

"Ooooo," her mother said. "If that's nothing, I'd hate to see your face when somebody walks over your grave."

This was not a settling thought, no matter how you looked at it.

Calm down, Nola urged herself. *No need to panic.* Nobody was likely to see the bucket set up where it was, or hear the sounds that came from it.

Not overnight, Nola berated herself. *Not for a few hours. Not for a day.*

But eventually.

Eventually.

How long before someone stumbled across it? The silversmith's new bride, perhaps, exploring every little corner of her new home?

Unlikely, Nola tried to convince herself. Innis's bride was starting a new life. There would be so much else to see, so many other demands on her time.

And time—Nola tried to reassure herself—might as easily be an ally as an enemy. There hadn't been that much water in the bucket. And—in one of those everyday kinds of magic no one could explain—water left out eventually went dry. How long would it take for this particular water to go away, taking the dancing shadowforms with it? A week? Two? Three? Four? The bride—Sulis was her name, Nola remembered—Sulis wouldn't even arrive for almost a week. And surely Brinna and Alan would be too busy with wedding preparations to notice a bucket with a bit of water in it beneath a rag under the stairs of the root cellar.

You're a fool, Nola told herself, *a fool. And you deserve whatever happens to you for being such a fool.*

But she didn't really believe that.

She became aware that her mother had put her arms around her. Her mother was rocking Nola, humming the same calming lullaby that she used for the baby in her forefinger. People were watching them with various expressions, the most friendly of which was wryly amused.

"I'm fine," Nola assured her. But of course she was lying.

✣ CHAPTER FIVE

Taverns were likely places to find work. On busy nights a tavern keeper was often happy to trade meals and a bed for help in preparing or serving food and drink, or for cleaning up. Even on slow nights many tavern keepers could be convinced to let someone eat what food was left over and sleep in the stable.

Of course, Nola knew from experience that tavern keepers were more eager to hire serving girls her own age than her mother's. And she told herself she was not in the least bitter that they were most eager of all to hire a serving girl if she had—for example—hair the color of ripening wheat, as Brinna did, rather than hair more the color of dried grass, the way certain other people did. Such a girl was likely to be popular among the men being served. With such a serving girl the men might stay longer and order more drinks, which would make the tavern keeper happy and more inclined to keep the girl on, and perhaps her odd mother, too. And men might give tips to such a girl, which she and her mother might save for leaner days.

But it also meant fighting—without looking as though you were fighting—to keep men's hands off you, and all in all Nola preferred not to put on a glamour of soft golden hair and a magically enhanced figure. Better to look like her own drab self—though her mother, of course, insisted she wasn't drab. But everyone knows mothers can't see straight when it comes to their daughters.

Nola and her mother stopped at a tavern with the unlikely—and, Nola thought, unlucky—name of the Witch's Stew. Still, it was well situated and appeared to be busy and lively. Almost every stool and bench was taken, and people were continually calling, "Edris, more mutton here," or "Edris, my cup is empty." Edris had to be the large but brisk and efficient woman who seemed to be in charge. The clamor itself was encouraging; even though the woman was handling things well, the pace had to be exhausting.

"Excuse me," Nola said in a moment of relative quiet. "Your name is Edris?" Not a brilliant opening, but adequate. Before the woman had a chance to say more than "Aye," Nola continued. "My mother and I, we've heard good things about your establishment—"

There was an old man she'd already noticed sitting in the corner by the hearth, his gnarled hands clutching a cane as though he was about to stand, though he looked too frail to get far. Now he showed he wasn't nearly as fragile as he looked; he thumped the cane on the floor and corrected her, "*My* establishment. I built this place with my own two hands when there was nothing here but a road through the forest."

The woman, Edris, rolled her eyes, though Nola couldn't guess why. "My father," Edris said, "Modig."

Whoever had built the place, Edris was obviously in charge now, but before Nola could continue talking to her, the old man went on: "This was after the floods in the south that came in the year of the pestilence, but before the war between the king and his brother, the one who had no sense about women."

Nola didn't know anything about the king, but she certainly thought she would have heard about a war. She wondered if the man was talking about the previous king. Still, she quickly saw she couldn't spend too much time trying to work out every specific thing that the tavern keeper's father said, because then she could never keep up. Already he was saying, "So I said to myself, 'Here I have been in the king's army'—because he had called us up to help in the city, what with the bodies stacking up faster than they could be buried, and the water rising, so of course he sent for Lord Gimm's men, of which I was one because my father had put me in service as he himself had a back that gave him trouble ever since he was a child, harking back to the time the barn door fell on him because his own father had been drinking the day he put the barn up, and—"

"Old man," Edris said calmly though firmly, "they're not interested."

43

"They asked," the old man protested.

"They did not," Edris told him. To Nola she added, "If you insist on being polite, I assure you smiling every once in a while and nodding is more than enough. Truly. He takes the fact that you're in the same room as encouragement. And if you leave the room, he'll call out after you to make sure you can hear from wherever it is you've gone."

"That's not true," the old man said. "Well, not all the time."

Edris continued, "The only way to get him to stop is to take his cane away from him and thump it on the floor and shout, 'Enough, old man.'"

Despite the fact that the words could have been harsh, the woman's tone was affectionate, so Nola did not feel at all sorry for the old man as he repeated sullenly, "It's my establishment," but simply recognized it as his determination to have the last word.

"Aye," the daughter agreed, "that it is, but I am the one to whom falls the day-to-day running of the tavern." Once more she gave her full attention to Nola. "What did you want to ask me?"

Just when it appeared that Nola would finally be able to state their business and learn if they had a place to spend the night, her mother spoke up. She asked Modig, "Was it the king who had no sense with women, or the king's brother who had no sense with women?"

"Ha!" the old man cried. "Either! Why, I remember a time—"

"Father!" Edris said in exasperation. "It makes no difference. They're both dead now, dead and gone."

"Well," Nola's mother said, to Nola's dismay, "of course, there's dead, and then there's dead and gone. And sometimes somebody starts out as one, and ends up the other, or sometimes it's the other way around."

"Exactly," Modig crowed triumphantly. "So there I was, fresh from my service to the king…"

Nola was desperately trying out different excuses she might use, but Edris waved her hand in a dismissive gesture at her father and Nola's mother, and she said to Nola, "It's good of your mother to humor the old man. So many of his friends are dead."

"I know," Nola answered earnestly, "*exactly* what you mean."

"Are you looking for work?" Edris asked. "Is that what I should take you to have been asking? If so, you're a godsend."

"We *are* looking for work," Nola said, amazed that twice in a row now she hadn't had to beg, or even to ask. Of course, she hoped this would turn out better than their short stay at the silversmith's house.

"If you can help me in here," Edris said, and then leaned closer to add, "and if your mother can keep my father from, well, from annoying the customers with his long-winded accounts of times past, this could work out well for both of us. You see"—she looked embarrassed to admit this— "I love him dearly. But he can actually drive customers away with his chattering about the old days.

And your mother looks to be—well, not his age, but closer to it than most of the people who come in here. My niece and her husband do most that needs doing in the kitchen. If your mother could help out, just a little, just light work, and once in a while—she doesn't even need to listen to the old man—maybe just nod occasionally and say, 'Yes, yes...'" Edris drifted off, looking as though she expected to be rebuffed.

"If nothing else," Nola assured her, "my mother is a very good listener."

✿ CHAPTER SIX

Nola spent the evening serving customers and smiling at customers and making sure customers didn't sneak away without paying. It seemed to drag on forever.

There was no longer any way for Nola to magically spy on the man who grew blackberries in Low Beck. Either he would come after her or not—and she would have no warning.

But in any case, that now seemed to have been worrying for the sake of worrying. A far greater problem was that the bespelled bucket of water would be discovered. And if she feared that a man would track her down a day-and-a-half's journey away to denounce her as a witch because she had hurt his pride and caused him to drop and break a jug, how relentless would the pursuit be if someone discovered a spell she had left in progress?

Keep moving, the most cautious part of her urged. *This town is too close by.*

But then she argued with herself, *It's not. You worry*

too much, and you'll yet be the death of both Mother and yourself by this constant fleeing.

Everything hinged on whether the bucket had been discovered or not.

Of course, there was one easy way to find out, for she had hairs from the silversmith's house. One was gray and might belong to Innis himself, or it might be from someone who had simply been in the shop, for she had found it on one of the pieces of velvet Innis used to display his finer wares. Then there were three long golden strands that were obviously Brinna's. And five light brown ones that could belong to either Kirwyn or Alan. Or rather, in all probability three of them were Kirwyn's because she had gotten them from his room when she had cleaned in there the first night; and the fourth was probably Alan's, for she had found that when she had—for that specific reason—offered to make up his bed in the cubbyhole by the stairs; and the last she had gotten off the kitchen floor, so that it could easily belong to either man. But all five were similar in color and length, and she had made no attempt when gathering them to keep track of which was which.

So, she decided, she would start with Brinna. For of them all Brinna was the one most likely to find reason to go down to the root cellar, where she might happen upon the bucket with the spell still going on inside it.

When she and her mother were at last in the privacy of the larder room where Edris had said they could set up beds, Nola cleared a space on one of the shelves so that she could place the washbasin there.

"Oh, no, not again," Nola's mother moaned when Nola poured out a pitcherful of water. "Leave be, Nola. Half the time it's precisely because you're so fretful things will go awry that you specifically *cause* things to go awry."

It didn't help Nola's mood that Nola suspected she might be right.

Nevertheless, Nola put her hands over the basin and said the magic words. Then she took a strand of Brinna's hair and dropped it into the water.

The shadowforms began to dance.

Brinna was in the kitchen, the day's pots and crocks and dishes cleaned and stacked neatly on the counter. Her blond hair was tied up, but with long strands hanging loose as she scrubbed vigorously at the floor. The bucket beside her was the bigger one she normally used, not the smaller one Nola had left in the root cellar.

Poor Brinna, Nola thought: still at work so late because there was no one to help her. There was a crock on the table that Nola knew, from her short time in the household, contained dried beans. Apparently there would be beans to eat tomorrow, and after Brinna finished scrubbing the floor she would measure out and sort the beans so that they could soak overnight.

Nola was determined to prove her mother wrong: She was *not* overly fretful; she would pluck Brinna's hair out of the water, and she would resist looking again until tomorrow. But even as her fingers broke the surface of the water, she saw something in the quiet domestic scene that made her pause.

Over Brinna's shoulder, framed by the unshuttered window, a man's face appeared.

Nola lifted her fingers out of the basin, and the water settled.

Kirwyn, she realized. But what was Kirwyn doing, standing outside his own house, staring in the window as Brinna washed the floor?

Nola hesitated, and in the bucket Brinna gave a sigh of weariness and reached to rub the small of her back. And Kirwyn absolutely proved he had no honest business being where he was: Seeing Brinna start to move, he ducked down below the sill of the window to avoid being seen.

He's spying on her, Nola thought. Of course, Nola was spying, too, but she knew why she was interested. What mischief was Kirwyn up to?

A moment later Brinna resumed scouring the floor. Sure enough, as Nola watched, Kirwyn peeked in again, warily, as though ready to dive for cover.

Nola became aware, in the world beyond the basin of bespelled water, that her mother was standing next to her, also watching what was happening.

"What's he doing?" Nola asked.

As though there could be no other answer, her mother said, "Hoping she'll get hot enough to loosen her bodice." Seeing Nola's look of startled distaste, she laughed and said, "Come to bed before you see something you *really* don't want to see."

No, Nola thought. *That isn't it.* Or, at least, that wasn't all of it. She doubted Kirwyn would mind if Brinna took off her top, but his look held more than the hope of catching a glimpse of a woman undressed. *He HATES her,* Nola thought. *He admires her beauty, but...* She shuddered at the hard look on Kirwyn's face.

To prove to her mother that she could do it, Nola plucked the hair out of the water; and when the ripples settled all she could see was the bottom of the basin.

Her mother sat on the edge of the mattress she and Nola had just finished stuffing and began to unfasten her shoes, first one, then the other, and still Nola stood by the washbasin. It was the way her mother gave such a knowing sigh and shook her head that settled the matter for her. If her mother knew she wasn't strong enough to resist, why bother fighting?

Nola looked at the five brown hairs, three—if not four—of which were Kirwyn's. She selected one and threw it into the basin. If it was Alan's, so be it. Whatever came, she was determined this would be the last spell tonight. The water, already bespelled, shivered.

It was Kirwyn's hair.

Kirwyn had left the kitchen window and was walking—in the dark—around the outside of the house. His steps were careful and precise, more so than he would need simply to avoid bumping into obstacles. He seemed to be trying to move without a sound. Dodging from shadow to shadow, he made his way toward the front of the house. He stopped once, crouched and silent, and waited while someone on the nearby street passed.

Well, at least he wasn't trying to sneak up on Brinna.

In fact, Nola saw he was heading toward the door that led into his father's shop.

Kirwyn waited until the street was empty, then he knocked against the door.

No answer.

Kirwyn stepped to the side of the shop and rapped his knuckles against the closed shutter.

Innis's voice came, very faintly, through the wood of the wall and the water of the spell. "Shop is closed. Come back tomorrow."

"This is important," Kirwyn hissed through the crack of the shutter. He went back to the door and knocked again.

The silversmith flung the door open. "What is it?" he said, and—before Kirwyn could answer—"You!" in a tone of surprise that indicated he hadn't recognized his son's voice through the urgent whispering at the shutter.

Light spilled onto the street. With one hand up to urge quiet, Kirwyn motioned with his other hand for his father to back into the shop. Innis, who had not seen Kirwyn's stealthy movements nor how he had waited until the street was empty, stepped backward. Kirwyn followed and hastily closed the door behind him.

Doesn't he see? Nola wondered of Innis. *Can't he tell something is wrong?*

In the room beyond the basin, Nola saw a movement out of the corner of her eye. Her mother reached forward, and Nola caught hold of her wrist before she could upset the basin.

Her mother began a high-pitched moan, though Nola knew she hadn't been rough enough to cause her mother harm.

"Stop it," Nola begged urgently. She let go, and her mother cradled her arm, rocking back and forth. The whining moan became a strangled-sounding hum—a lullaby to calm the baby in her forefinger.

Nola looked away from her mother and back to the basin.

On the shelf behind the silversmith's workbench were several silver cups, ornaments, a knife handle, buckles. The back door leading to the silversmith's bedroom was open. On one of the tables was a small but high-edged wooden tray on which were other silver items. By chance or design, Kirwyn had caught Innis in the process of putting valuables away for the night, locking them in the more secure inner room.

"What *is* it, Kirwyn?" Innis demanded.

"I found myself locked out," Kirwyn said, "and Brinna and Alan already to bed. I didn't want to disturb them."

"So you disturb me, instead?" Innis turned away in disgust and picked up the tray he had obviously set down

53

to answer the summons at the door. Over his shoulder he added, "And if the servants are abed at this hour, they obviously are not kept busy enough."

Instead of following his father into the inner room, Kirwyn went to the largest of the silversmith's several anvils. His hand hovered over the tools beside it, then he selected a hammer, the biggest of them, a tool apparently meant for the earliest, roughest work.

Nola's mother, standing the length of the room away from Nola and the basin, became more frantic in her humming.

Turn around! Nola mentally warned the silversmith. But, of course, nothing she did on this side of the water could affect the scene she viewed. Nola wished she had let her mother tip out the water. *She* wanted to tip out the water, but in her horror she couldn't move. She didn't want to see what was coming, what she knew was coming. *Turn around! Turn around!*

Innis didn't turn around.

Kirwyn followed his father into the bedroom. There was a second door that led to the rest of the house, but this was closed. The silversmith had his back turned. He crouched down to lift a section of boards from the floor and removed a wooden chest from the cavity there and set it on the bed. He was fitting a key into the lock, obviously intent on putting his silver away securely for the night, too intent to notice that he was not alone.

Kirwyn raised his arm.

Perhaps his father saw the shadow fall across the box. Still crouched, he turned. "No!" he cried.

Kirwyn brought the hammer down on top of his father's head.

The silversmith fell back against the bed, the heavy box crashing to the floor an instant after his body did.

The whole washbasin seemed to take on the color of the spilled blood. Nola imagined she could smell it. Her head swam and she put her arm out to keep from falling. The basin went off the back of the shelf and crashed to the floor, shattering, taking water, and hair, and murdered silversmith with it.

In the silence of the tavern room, Nola heard her mother murmur, "I told her to leave it. I did tell her."

✣ CHAPTER SEVEN

Nola could hear footsteps hurrying down the hall. "Don't say a word," she whispered urgently to her mother.

Her mother threw her arms up in exasperation. "Why should I say anything?" she asked. "Nobody ever listens anyway."

There was a rapping at their door—uncommon courtesy to people in their situation—and Edris called out, "Is anything amiss in there?"

Nola opened the door. "I'm so sorry," she told the tavern keeper, gesturing to indicate the broken washbasin. The spilled water looked, once more, like water, rather than blood. "I was trying to get everything settled just so, and I pushed the basin too far in and it just went over the back edge."

Edris looked only mildly annoyed. "Ah, well," she said. "Accidents do happen. I hope you're better with trays of food and drink than you are with washbasins."

"I'll be very careful," Nola assured her.

Edris's ancient father, Modig, was shuffling his way down the hall also, to see what the excitement was. "Crashes," he said. "Alarms in the night. We haven't had such a commotion since that time that man tried to sneak the goat into his room."

Edris ignored her father. "It's only…" She glanced to Nola's mother, who had sat back down on the bed, hugging herself and rocking.

She heard us arguing, Nola thought. *She's trying to decide if we're likely the kind of people who throw things when we get angry with each other.*

Modig finally made it to the doorway. "This," he said, "reminds me of the time—"

"Father!" Edris snapped. Looking straight at Nola's mother, she asked her, "*Is* everything all right?"

Nola's mother covered her mouth, one hand over the other, and said through the cracks between her fingers, "I'm not allowed to say."

"She's joking," Nola said to Edris's aghast expression. "Mother likes to tease."

Edris raised one eyebrow skeptically.

Nola sighed. "Actually, that isn't true." *She probably suspects I beat Mother regularly,* Nola judged. She said, "What really happened is that my mother just gave me some bad news. Something she should have told me this morning, before we ever came to Saint Erim Turi."

"Very bad news," Nola's mother echoed agreeably. "Death." She nodded. Then she tightened her hands over her mouth as though the words weren't already out.

"Yes," Nola said, before her mother decided to say anything worse. "Someone we know died."

"Oh, I'm so sorry." Edris made the sign of the cross.

Her father did, too. He said, "I knew a man once who died—"

Nola continued, interrupting, determined to convince Edris that she hadn't been throwing the room's furnishings about. "I was so upset, I wasn't paying attention, and that's when I accidentally set the basin too far back and it fell. Off the back. Behind the shelves." She realized she was repeating herself. And showing a tendency to babble. But still, she moved to stand by the shelves—as though Edris couldn't find them on her own—and she indicated the basin behind the shelves and hoped Edris realized how unlikely a throw would have been needed to make the basin end up back there. "Right before *that* happened I was just telling my mother—not shouting, of course, but just maybe raising my voice, just to be heard across the length of the room—that now we would have to go back—"

"Not *back*!" Nola's mother cried, finally taking her hands down completely from over her mouth so that she could pull on her hair. "Nola, what are you thinking? And here I was, afraid that you would be wanting to go *forward*. Again. As if that wasn't bad enough. But of course not. 'Here's a nice, safe, friendly place in Saint Erim Turi,' my Nola says to herself. 'I know what we should do: We should *leave*, as soon as we get here, that's the only sensible thing to do.' Naturally." She struck herself on the side of the head. "Why didn't I think of that?"

"Mother!" Nola warned. To Edris, she said, "Mother is a bit overwrought. She's thinking of the sadness of the situation, and not taking into account that in this time of sorrow our poor friends shouldn't have to concern themselves with day-to-day household tasks, in which we could help them."

Edris was watching Nola's mother. From behind Edris, and from over Modig's shoulder, Nola made frantic faces at her mother that were meant to convey that she wasn't really thinking of going back to Haymarket, and would her mother, please, just for once, play along? Going back was only a pretext. For what would Edris and Modig think of them if Nola had said, "Somebody in the last town we visited has died, and now we must move on from here because we're only a day's journey away"? It made sense that people who knew each other would come together in times of bereavement. If her mother would only realize *going back* was a ruse and stop making such a fuss. It was hard enough to think.

Modig said, "You try to go back, and you try to go back." He thumped his cane and shook his head. "But you never can."

What was going on at the silversmith's house—even now as her mother craned around Edris and asked Nola, "What is it you're trying to tell me, dear? I can't make it out from the faces you're making."

"Nothing," Nola said. "I'm trying not to cry over the death of our poor friend."

Surely, she thought, Kirwyn wasn't stupid. He couldn't expect to bash his father across the head and get away with it. Was his plan to kill the servants, too, and claim an intruder had broken in? Or would he try to set the blame on Brinna or Alan?

On Brinna, Nola thought, remembering Kirwyn's face through the kitchen window, and the hate she had seen there.

But then she went even colder than she had when she'd realized she was about to witness a murder.

Or on us, she thought.

How much more likely was it for Kirwyn to blame Nola and her mother for the death? Had he, in fact, already discovered the bespelled bucket in the basement? "Obviously witchcraft," he would say to the authorities, showing them the shadowform of a living man in a bucket of water. And he could claim...what? That the figure they could see had stepped out of the bucket and killed the silversmith? *They* wouldn't know that was impossible, that Nola didn't have—and would never use, even if she did have—that kind of magic. And they would know that she was the one who had set up the spell—who else was there who could have done it? Who had recently had access to the silversmith's basement, besides Brinna and Alan? And *they* had lived in Haymarket all their lives, and everybody knew they weren't witches.

Who but the two strangers, who had been asked to leave precisely for being so strange?

And if what she had been afraid of came to pass, and the blackberry merchant from Low Beck tracked her down to Haymarket, or if somebody from Haymarket recognized his shadowform and the authorities tracked *him* down, that would not exonerate her. He would be able to protect himself. "I was at home with my family, with my field workers," he would tell them. "That creature that the witch created and placed in the bucket has a separate life from me, so I am not responsible for its crimes. She is. I always said she was a witch."

And even if—if—Kirwyn hadn't discovered the bucket and had a different plan to evade being found out, then someone—the town magistrate or representatives from the lord who held this land—would come to investigate the crime. And *they* would find the bucket. That bucket might have been—*might* have been—safe from discovery long enough to go dry if all that was going on in the silversmith's house was a wedding. But it would certainly be chanced upon now that there had been murder done.

She and her mother would have to leave—now, tonight, immediately—and flee farther and faster than they ever had before.

She became aware that Edris had taken hold of her arm, and she jerked away, thinking that somehow Edris knew, Edris was trying to restrain her, Edris planned to hand her over to the Saint Erim Turi authorities. But Edris didn't try to catch hold of her again. She only said, mildly, "Sometimes it's best to weep and not hold it in." And Nola realized she was responding to the last thing Nola had said, that Nola was trying not to cry over a supposed friend's death.

Modig said, "You try to hold it in, and you try to hold it in. But you can't."

Nola sat down heavily, just barely making it onto the straw-filled mattress on the floor.

Edris—for all her bulk and despite being at least twice Nola's age—crouched down beside her. "I'm so sorry," she said, so sympathetically—over the wrong thing—that Nola found herself crying.

She and her mother would never, she knew, *absolutely never,* be able to outrun the storm that would break out in Haymarket if that bucket was discovered. She said, and this time she meant it, "We must go back." If the bucket hadn't been seen yet, she must make sure it never was.

Her mother said, "None of us thinks you should go."

Edris, misunderstanding, thinking that Nola's mother was including *her* in the sentiment, said, "I don't know." She shook her head, to indicate she didn't know the situation, and in truth she *didn't* know the situation, much more than she could ever guess. Still, she pointed a finger at her father to warn him not to take sides, and she repeated, unwilling to get between mother and daughter, "I don't know."

Annoyed with herself, Nola wiped her eyes. They *had* to go back. Yet how could they—when she knew Kirwyn had already killed once? How could they go back when everyone would blame her mother because they had all heard her say that Innis would die?

That thought made Nola's mind stop going in the same circle. How had her mother known? Of course. Some abbot had told her, some abbot who had found his way into her mother's head. Well, he hadn't exactly told her. Her mother had overheard him saying the Mass for the Dead. But since when had her mother's voices been real—never mind been able to tell the future?

It was a coincidence, Nola told herself. An awful coincidence that could get the two of them killed. The *three* of them, she wryly corrected herself, if you counted the abbot.

And surely she would be as mad as her mother if she took her mother back to Haymarket. It would take twice as long to get there, and people would be twice as apt to notice them, and things were twice as likely to go awry.

But Nola had to go there.

And how could she *not* take her mother? What other choice was there—to leave her here?

Nola looked at Edris and Modig, who had come running—well, come as fast as each of them could—when they thought there was some trouble, who had asked pointed questions to make sure Nola's mother was not being harmed, who were—contrary to all expectation—friendly.

I can't leave her here, Nola thought. *What would she say, what would she do, what trouble would she get into without me?*

But it was safer than taking her to Haymarket. Wasn't it? Where both a murderer and the authorities were?

It was a *terrible* plan. But there was no other choice.

To her mother, she said, "I can travel much faster alone." To Edris, she said, "Would you…Could it be possible…Is there any way—"

"I would very much like for your mother to stay here," Edris said, as though the idea had come to her first, "if that would be convenient for you. My father so much enjoyed talking to her this evening."

Modig thumped his cane. "Listens better than anybody. I haven't met such a good listener since the old blacksmith died."

Edris said, "You mean Deaf Harold?"

"The very one," Modig agreed.

Nola's mother got a distant expression on her face. "Harold," she said thoughtfully. "Harold…"

Nola rested her face in her hands, but in the end her mother said, "No. No Deaf Harold. Of course, there *is* Abbot Dinsmore, whose hearing isn't very good, on account of all those monastery bells ringing."

"I think," Nola announced to everyone, "it would be best if I start tonight."

"But it's dark out," Edris protested.

That was the whole point. Nola hoped to get to Haymarket before the new day started, before things went too far. "It will be best this way," she assured Edris.

Edris shook her head but didn't argue "Let me pack a breakfast for you."

It was the second time in a very long day that someone had taken trouble to see that she would have a meal. She was unaccustomed to the concern. "Thank you," she said.

As she followed Edris out of the room, she heard Modig tell her mother, "I knew an abbot once who was so determined to prove he was the holiest man in Christendom that…"

And Nola hurriedly shut the door behind her.

✡ CHAPTER EIGHT

Nola planned to walk all night. But two days of almost steady walking and near-constant fear, separated by only one short night of rest in the silversmith's house, had left her drained. And obviously, she chided herself as she accidentally strayed off the path and stepped calf-deep into a cold stream, making one bad decision after another. Her legs wobbling under her. It would be safer, she told herself, to rest during the darkest part of the night. Arriving in Haymarket at dawn couldn't be that much better than arriving midmorning, while arriving too exhausted to think straight would be considerably worse.

As she lay down in a grassy hollow formed between the massive roots of a huge oak, she just hoped that the situation wasn't already far beyond what she and her wits could handle.

✡

When she awoke it was dawn, which was later than she had planned, and it was raining.

Last chance, she told herself, as her skirt flapped in the wind. *This is the last sensible time to change your mind and go back to the tavern, fetch Mother, and make a run for it.*

But she still couldn't convince herself that running *was* a sensible plan.

Crouched under the shelter of the tree—which wasn't much shelter at all—she ate the sliced mutton and bread that Edris had packed for her. As the ground under her feet melted into mud, she heard from the nearby road the rattle of a wagon coming from the direction of Saint Erim Turi, headed toward Haymarket. For the moment she and the wagon were still separated by a slight rise in the road.

Surely if it was *sensible* she was after, it was better to ride than to walk, even if the rain *was* beginning to lessen.

Nola took from her bodice the piece of wool that still contained the hairs she had collected at the silversmith's house. The gray one, Innis's, she would never use now. But there were still two of Brinna's, at least one of Alan's, and two, possibly three, of Kirwyn's—not that she was eager to look in on Kirwyn again. But she *might* need the hairs—who knew what the future might bring?—so she set aside the wool to keep them out of the range of the spell she was about to cast.

Then, still crouched down, she wrapped her arms about herself and said the magic words that would shift her appearance. She chose to look like a young boy, feeling that was probably safer—out in the countryside alone among strangers—than being a young woman, even a rather plain young woman. She made herself look like a skinny twelve-year-old boy, and made her clothes look like mud- and grass-stained, slightly too small, much-patched boys' clothing. There was no sense in looking like anyone who might have something worth stealing. She shoved the wet square of wool with the hairs in it into her shirt and managed to scramble back up onto the road just as the wagon crested the hill.

The driver was alone—a farmer, judging by his cartload of geese and pigs and goats, on his way to market. The cart was pulled by a horse that looked almost as old as Edris's father, but all in all they were still moving faster than Nola would have cared to walk. None of them—farmer, horse, geese, pigs, or goats—looked any happier about the day than Nola was.

"Hello," Nola called out, her voice altered by the same spell that had changed her appearance. "Are you going to Haymarket? And are you interested in company along the road?"

"I *am* on my way to Haymarket," the farmer said, slowing but not stopping, "and running late because of this rain so that I'm cranky for it, and used anyway to traveling on my own, so I'm not especially looking for company." But then he relented. "You needing a ride?"

"That I am," Nola admitted, though by that time she was shouting to his back.

The man pulled on the reins and stopped the wagon. "Then climb up," he said.

The rain stopped, eventually, and they arrived at Haymarket when it was still morning. The market area, though puddled and dripping, was busy, with housewives and servants going from stall to stall. But it was late to be just setting up. The only saving grace for the farmer was that the rain had delayed everything.

"Thank you," Nola called as the man found his place and unfastened the horse from its harness. Though that was just about the full extent of their conversation— "Please take me to Haymarket" and "Thank you"—he told her as she jumped off the cart, "If you want a ride back to where I picked you up, be here again by noon."

"Thank you," Nola repeated, delighted. Noon. Surely that was time enough to find her way—although she did not know *how*—back into the silversmith's house. Of course, she had no idea who would be there, or how many people Kirwyn had killed over the night—but surely until noon was long enough to stop the spell that she had stupidly left going for two days now.

So. She had no plan, but at least she had a way to leave.

That was better than nothing.

She hoped.

She kept the form of a young boy as she made her way among the market stalls, her ears alert to any talk of what had happened the night before. Normally market

69

vendors might have been suspicious of a boy looking like Nola, a boy who obviously had nothing, and many would have told him to be off, afraid that his intention was to grab something and flee with it into the crowd. But today everybody was too busy talking, for the news was fresh and shocking: Master Innis was dead, killed— so everyone said—by an intruder, who had stolen the contents of the silversmith's strongbox, but had then been run off the property by the dead man's son.

Oh, for goodness' sake, Nola thought in exasperation. How had Kirwyn pulled *that* off? Still, it was none of her business.

She was happy to gather from what she overheard that Brinna and Alan had *not* been murdered, nor apparently was anyone blaming the two servants of the house for the murder. And she was happier still to hear nothing about a bucket, or witchcraft, or a pair of serving women who had been dismissed earlier on the same day of the killing. She was not happy to learn that word had been sent to Lord Pendaran, whose estates included the town of Haymarket, and that the lord had sent one of his minor lordlings to seek out more details of the crime.

So. Someone was asking questions and looking around.

But surely he wouldn't be looking around the root cellar, she told herself. Not so soon.

Or would he? One of the things Nola learned was that the silversmith's money was missing: The silver he had fashioned into jewelry and trinkets was still there, scattered about the floor and his body. But the strongbox was opened—indicating the silversmith had been compelled to show the thief where his money and unworked silver was hidden—and now it was empty. Yet Innis had shouted out in alarm just as the killer struck him. The question that seemed to be on everybody's lips was, How had the intruder, carrying all that money, gotten out of the house, out of the yard, and off the street so fast?

Nola knew there had been no intruder, but she also wondered, briefly, what Kirwyn had managed to do—before witnesses began arriving—with the contents of the strongbox. But a more important question was, What would this Lord Pendaran's agent assume the killer had done with the missing money? Everyone seemed convinced the murderer was an outsider; but, still, Nola guessed, a thorough search would have to include the silversmith's yard. A very thorough search might include the house.

What if the house had been searched already? What if she was already too late?

Nola began to seek out a place where she could be alone to work a spell, so that she could magically peek into the house to see what was happening, see if it was safe to return. There were certainly enough puddles from the night's rain. All she had to do was find one behind something, or in an out-of-the-way corner, or—

She was so busy craning her neck to see between the vendors' stalls that she walked into someone.

"Excuse me," she mumbled, still searching the ground off to the side.

"It's all right," said a voice she recognized. "But it's easier to see where you're going if your eyes and your feet are pointed in the same direction."

Nola looked up and found herself facing Brinna.

"I— I'm sorry," Nola stammered.

"It's all right," Brinna repeated. She smiled to show she really meant it, and for a moment Nola forgot that Brinna couldn't recognize her and saw only a ragged and dirty twelve-year-old boy, a clumsy stranger.

Seeing Brinna's familiar and friendly face, Nola had to fight the inclination to blurt out, "I need to talk to you. I know who killed Innis, and I fear your life is in danger, too. Please trust me." But Nola herself trusted no one. How could she ask someone to have faith in her? She had spent too much of her life hiding secrets.

And then the moment was gone. One of the three young women clustered around Brinna elbowed Nola out of the way. "We were *talking*," this one sneered, in that tone used solely by irate young women between the ages of thirteen and twenty to boys too young to be worth notice.

One of the others tugged on Brinna's arm, almost causing her to upend the basket in which she carried the items she had bought in the market, turnips and onions being what Nola caught a glimpse of. Brinna's friend demanded of Brinna, "Tell us about this man Galvin that Lord Pendaran sent."

Brinna turned away from Nola and answered, "I told you. He's asking about last night—"

"I don't mean *that*," the woman said. "I mean, what's he like?" And before Brinna could do more than open her mouth, the woman continued. "Reaghan says he's *very* attractive."

Brinna laughed. "Reaghan should know. She nearly fell out of the window trying to get a better look."

Reaghan must have been the one with the pointy elbows. She looked down her nose at the others and said, "Well, he was worth the risk. He has beautiful eyes."

"He does have kind eyes," Brinna agreed.

"And a very nice smile," Reaghan added.

"And *many* questions," Brinna said, indicating— Nola thought—more sense than all three of her friends combined.

The third friend said, "I don't know. If he looks as good as Reaghan says, I'd let him ask me all the questions he wanted, and I'd admit to anything for him."

Empty-headed fools, Nola thought. She'd heard accounts of how witches were questioned, and she didn't find amusing the thought of being willing to admit to anything.

Nola couldn't just continue to stand on the fringe of the group, hoping to pick up information about what had happened last night. Any moment now one of Brinna's friends was sure to comment on street urchins who eavesdropped on the conversations of their betters. Besides, they were only eager to hear about the man who

73

had been sent to inquire about the murder. Apparently they had learned earlier all they wanted to about the murder itself. Reluctant as Nola was to separate herself from the one friend she had in Haymarket, she drifted away from the four young women.

Almost at the end of the row of vendors, she found a spot behind one of the stalls that was awkward to get to, and was shielded from easy view. Best of all, it included a nice puddle. Nola took out her square of wool that held the hairs. *Let this be Alan's,* she hoped. She hated the thought of seeing Kirwyn, dreading that she might accidentally witness him killing someone else, unlikely as that was.

Nola glanced around to make sure the place was truly as deserted as it seemed, then she whispered the magic words and tossed the curliest of the brown hairs into the muddy water.

To her relief, Alan's form appeared in the puddle, standing in the silversmith's shop. He had his arms crossed over his chest and he looked both nervous and guilty about something. Nola could sympathize; she, too, had a tendency to look guilty when anything went wrong, even if she had nothing to do with it.

It turned out Kirwyn was there, too, after all, looking puffy-eyed and distraught. *Liar,* Nola thought.

And then there was one more man, who had to be the one sent by Lord Pendaran, for she could tell by his clothing that he was neither artisan nor simple townsman come to join the household in mourning. Lord Galvin, the young women had said. Nola probably wouldn't have noticed if Brinna's friends hadn't made such a fuss—for she didn't think people's appearances were what was important—but she supposed he *was* good looking, and Nola decided to hold that against him. In contrast to Alan's air of threatened anxiety and Kirwyn's act of grieving son, Galvin looked mostly tired and impatient. So, Nola thought, someone else who was already half exhausted this morning from having traveled through the night and been caught in the rain. She had no sympathy to spare for him. He was young, which hinted at a lack of experience in dealing with murder. Which could mean good or ill as far as Nola was concerned. On principle, she concluded it probably meant ill.

Alan was talking, and because his voice was quiet and there was noise from the street by the market stalls, the water didn't carry his words to Nola.

Lord Pendaran's man spoke more confidently, and his voice was clear. He said, "So when you ran into the serving girl—"

"Brinna," Alan said, and Nola caught from the other's expression that he had already been told the name and could remember it on his own, thank you, being the clever person he was, in a lord's employ and not just some servant in a silversmith's household.

"When you ran into Brinna," Galvin repeated, in a tone that could have been patience or condescension, "it was on the hall side of Master Innis's bedroom door, and she had not yet opened the door?"

Apparently this was a reiteration of something Alan had said, and Alan didn't immediately recognize it as a question. "Yes," he said, just as Galvin gave up waiting and urged, "Is that correct?"

As though working to rouse himself from his grief, Kirwyn said, "She should be back from marketing soon." He turned to Alan to complain. "You had no authority to give her permission to go. I always told my father you were next to useless."

Alan said, "I thought Lord Galvin was finished with the questions he was asking her."

Galvin didn't answer.

Kirwyn started to say something else, but Nola ran her hand through the puddle, dragging the hair out over the edge to end the spell. It was time to stop watching and act.

She had to get into the silversmith's house, and she knew that Brinna was out among the market stalls telling everyone what had happened, and Kirwyn, Alan, and Lord Pendaran's man were in the shop. There might not be a better time. She climbed out over the guide rope that held the awning over the stall and made her way toward the street where the silversmith lived. Had lived.

If she was lucky, she would be in and out of the house in the time it would take to make up a bed and not a person would notice her. But just in case some neighbor *did* see her entering through the kitchen door, she had better look like someone who had a right to be there. She didn't want to look like a stranger, for fear of shouts of "The intruder came back!" Nor should she look like herself, for that could be even worse if anyone recognized her as the one who had come around here two days ago seeking work—the strange one, with the stranger mother, who had been asked to leave.

So, while no plan seemed safe, the least dangerous was to look like Brinna, because Nola knew for a fact that Brinna was away in the market and that the curious people of Haymarket would likely keep her there for much longer than Nola needed.

So as she rounded the last corner she dropped the glamour that made her look like a boy and took on one that made her look like Brinna.

Nola opened the door and stepped into the kitchen.

And found a man in there, a soldier by the look of him, poking among the pots and crocks. "Hello again, Brinna," he said when he saw Nola. "Everybody's waiting for you in the shop."

✿ CHAPTER NINE

Stories flooded into Nola's memory of witches captured: stories told to her by her mother as warnings, and tales told by people who didn't know Nola was a witch and who shared their accounts as entertainment, or to satisfy themselves that honest folk always won out in the end over monsters and demons and witches and other such evil creatures.

Nola took a step back, and the soldier caught hold of her arm, firmly though not roughly. He must have seen she was close to panic, for he spoke reassuringly, as someone might to a skittish horse, "Easy there, now. I mean you no harm."

He didn't look especially cruel, but neither had the children in one village whom she had seen throw rocks at an old woman, an old woman who had evoked their suspicion because she shook and twitched and had a film over one eye.

Nola tried to pull free, thinking that if she could just get to the door...

If she got to the door, he would follow her.

And she couldn't pull free in any case. He didn't even have to strain to hold on to her.

"What is it, girl?" the soldier asked. He must be with that man Galvin, she collected herself enough to surmise, one of Lord Pendaran's guard. And very obviously he had already spoken once with the real Brinna.

So far he was being solicitous of her trembling and obvious fear. Nola estimated that wouldn't last long before he started to wonder just why she was so anxious when Brinna would know that he had cause to be here.

She let her free hand flutter over her heart, to acknowledge that she had been frightened, and gave a ragged half-laugh, half-sigh to show that now she was over it and embarrassed at her foolishness. "I'm sorry," she said. "You startled me. For a moment I didn't know who you were and I thought…" She forced herself to remember the sight of Kirwyn bringing the hammer down on his father's head, which caused her to shudder, which would have to be Brinna's reaction, too. She shook her head. "It was silly of me."

"Not at all," the man said, though his face indicated he thought it was *very* silly of her. He nodded toward the hall. "Lord Galvin is in the shop with Master Kirwyn, and he's eager to speak to you, to hear in more detail your account of what happened."

He still had his hand on Nola's arm, probably less to hold on to her than to indicate that he wanted her to keep moving. But even if he let go, Nola realized, she would never be able to dash to the door, open the latch, run into the courtyard, keep running around to the street, and lose him in a town she barely knew. She would have to do what he said: go talk to this man Galvin.

Take your time, she wished at Brinna. The last thing she needed was to have the real Brinna come home. *Tell EVERYBODY in the market EVERYTHING.*

Still, what kind of situation was she putting Brinna into? Once Nola escaped and Brinna came back, what then? She could just imagine these men of Lord Pendaran's saying to Brinna, "But the last time you were here you said..."

But what could Nola do besides go along with this for now?

The only way to get to the shop without going back outside was to go through Innis's room. Nola wasn't aware of balking until the soldier tightened his grip on her arm. She had no idea what to expect: Would the body still be there, lying in a pool of blood?

It was, and it wasn't.

Innis had been moved from the floor, but he was definitely still in the room. That had to be him on the bed, even though his body had been covered with a blanket. Nola hastily looked away and her gaze went to the floor, to the section that could be taken up—under which Innis had hidden his strongbox, and by which he had died. Someone—most probably Brinna—had worked hard to clean up the blood. Innis's bedroom was the only one in the house that had a wood floor, and the disadvantage of wood over rushes or a rug was that you couldn't just pick up what was soiled and replace it with fresh. The blood had soaked into the wood and seeped into the cracks, and even now there was a stain that could have been a residue of the blood itself or perhaps just a water spot where Brinna had soaked the floor while trying to get the blood up. Whether the stain was blood or water, the smell of blood still hung in the heavy air.

"Don't look," the soldier told her, which was good advice even if she was supposed to be the one who had cleaned up Innis's blood.

They entered the silversmith's shop. Even though everybody looked up when the two of them entered the room, the soldier introduced her, sounding as though she was receiving an audience: "The maid, Brinna, is back."

Pendaran's man Galvin smiled at her. Nobody, she thought, had ever been that pleased to see her when she looked like herself. "Hello," he said, immediately walking away from the other two men.

Nola was totally aware of her appearance. Brinna was a very attractive young woman, and Nola was sure that accounted for the considerate attention she was getting, first from the soldier, now from Galvin. *If it was me,* she thought, *with hair as limp and straight as dead and dried grass, the other one would have said, "Come on, then, snap out of it," and this one wouldn't be so quick to smile at me.*

Well, maybe he would have. They had Innis's ledger open, and Nola guessed Galvin and Kirwyn and Alan had been in the middle of trying to take an inventory, to determine if any of the silver had been stolen. Even now Kirwyn and Alan continued to debate whether the woman's bracelet with the embossed cross was missing or if it had been sold or if Master Innis had melted it down and made it into another item. Spend long enough doing that, she had to admit, and Galvin would have been sincerely relieved to see anyone.

"Well, it's about time," Kirwyn said to her. "Did you feel you had all day to loiter about the market, gossiping, keeping everyone waiting for you?" He made to step past Galvin.

Without even turning to face him, Galvin put his hand up, a definite "Enough, and step no further" gesture.

Kirwyn was used to more respect. He stopped, but scowled at Galvin's back.

Nola realized she was clinging to the soldier's arm when Galvin said, very seriously, as one might to a child, "Truly, I very rarely bite."

She forced herself to smile. But couldn't resist saying, "Nor do I. Usually."

His smile almost broadened, but he fought it, perhaps thinking the situation too serious for levity: talking to a woman who had discovered her employer only moments after he had been murdered. She remembered Brinna saying he had kind eyes. Were they? Hard to tell. They were gray and his hair—Nola had a tendency to notice hair—dark brown. He was probably used to women making a fuss over him, so she decided to like the soldier better, though he looked twice Galvin's age and not quite so clean.

As though to explain to Galvin why she was so apprehensive, the soldier said, "I gave Brinna quite a start in the kitchen. For a moment she thought I was the killer come back."

Galvin's attention, which had gone from Nola to the soldier, snapped back to Nola again. "Does Sergeant Halig bear a resemblance to the man who killed the silversmith?" he asked.

Sergeant Halig. Now she wouldn't have to ask, "What did you say your name was again?" and hope that he *had* introduced himself to Brinna. But as far as resembling Innis's killer…"No," Nola said, for Kirwyn was younger, shorter, and smaller than Halig, with hair that was longer and darker than Halig's, which could almost have been called blond.

"How close a look did you get?"

Nola realized her mistake at once. Brinna *had* said Galvin was full of questions. "Well, not very close," she admitted. How could she come out and accuse Kirwyn without revealing herself? Even pretending she was Brinna didn't work. What could she say? *I saw Kirwyn kill his father, only I didn't say anything about it last night, and I stayed in the house overnight because I knew that Kirwyn hadn't seen me see him, and I was waiting for you to*

come so that I could tell all to you, except I didn't tell any-
body else because I didn't want Kirwyn to have a chance to
run away or to kill me, and then once you DID come, I took
the first opportunity to get away from you because I ab-
solutely needed to do the marketing. Galvin might look too
young to have much experience in this sort of thing, but
he didn't look that gullible. And what would happen
when she left and the real Brinna came back and denied
saying it at all?

"But," Galvin prompted, gentle but insistent, "you
were close enough to see he didn't look like Halig?"

Nola considered, then decided that couldn't get her
into trouble. "Yes," she said.

And what was *that* expression that flickered across his
face? Was he amused at her, or just trying to appear
friendly and not frightening? He was definitely waiting
for her to say more. What had Brinna seen? What was
Brinna telling people in the market? It would be better for everyone, later on, if their stories matched. If
only Nola could say enough, without putting herself or
Brinna into trouble, to get Galvin to take notice of Kirwyn. She said, "I saw him only for an instant. From the
back, as he was running away."

She caught the quick flicker of surprise in Galvin's
eyes. He'd been paying attention before, but now he was
scrutinizing her. She'd just said something wrong. Then
it came to her: This was more than he expected. She
remembered when she had looked into the bespelled

puddle and she had heard Galvin talking to Alan. Galvin had asked whether Alan and Brinna opened the door leading into Innis's bedroom together. And Alan had said yes. They would have seen the same thing. She glanced at Alan, wondering what he'd said, what Brinna had said earlier and was now still saying in the market. Had either of them seen anything at all? Alan, she decided, looked surprised by her statement. She looked back at Galvin and realized that he'd seen her glance away from him. He didn't look over his shoulder, but surely he knew where everybody was standing.

She said, "I just saw the back of his head." Even that could be too much. "There was just the fleeting impression of brown hair, maybe a smaller build." What if they didn't suspect Kirwyn? What if they were so convinced it was an intruder that they found someone else, some poor innocent, who matched her description? She said, "But I may be wrong. It happened so fast and the light wasn't good. And I could see Master Innis on the floor, dead, and I was frightened, and distressed, and…" She was babbling again. She finished. "Confused."

Galvin asked, "Could you tell he was dead right away, or did you need to check?"

What in the world was he asking? And what was the right answer? "I…hoped…he wasn't."

Which they both realized wasn't an answer.

Behind Galvin, Alan said, "*I* checked to see if he was breathing. He was not."

It would help, Nola thought, if she could guess what was wrong, for something obviously was, though Galvin said nothing.

Kirwyn said, "He was definitely dead by the time I got there."

Nola fought to keep her face from showing amazed revulsion that he could say such a thing.

"And the silver?" Galvin asked her.

That she had learned in the market. "Scattered on the bed and floor," she answered confidently.

Kirwyn added, "Just as we've all told you before."

Galvin ignored him. "Did you notice anything missing—besides the money?"

And *that* she didn't know. She hoped he hadn't asked Brinna the same thing earlier. "I can't be sure *nothing* was taken," she said.

Kirwyn sighed. "I know we are all distraught over the terrible thing that has happened to my father, but that is no reason to be heedless. We must try to remember details so that Lord Galvin can finish here quickly and find the man who did this."

"Exactly," Galvin said, despite Kirwyn's implication that he was wasting time. If he was being sarcastic, Nola thought, it didn't come through in his voice. He said, "Sergeant Halig, please help Master Kirwyn and Alan continue to check the books against what's here. Perhaps I will get things straight in my mind better if Brinna showed me about the house."

At last, the opportunity to get down to the root cellar. Of course, it would only work if she made sure she got there at least two steps ahead of him. And if she could only be sure all he wanted was to see the house.

Alan asked, "Are you feeling unwell, Brinna? You look..." He shook his head and didn't finish with any of the things Nola felt and knew she probably looked: worried, unsteady, afraid she might vomit from fear.

Instantly Halig moved to put himself between Alan and Nola, to prevent Alan from joining them. *He* knew Galvin wanted to be alone with her.

Galvin didn't take her arm, as Halig had earlier, but only motioned for her to precede him. He did, however, repeat what his sergeant had said, "I mean you no harm."

No, Nola thought. *You just want to get me away from the others.* At best that might mean he wanted to see if separated from Alan and Kirwyn she gave the same answers to his questions. But under the circumstances even that wasn't good.

"Sir," Halig said, and stepped aside to whisper something into Galvin's ear.

Galvin nodded, giving no indication of whether he was pleased, dismayed, or surprised by whatever his sergeant told him.

He just gestured to Nola to indicate for her to start moving.

Anxious to get to the bucket, anxious to get away from Alan in case he wanted to dispute her version of what had happened, Nola started moving. "Where did you want to look?" she asked as they walked into Innis's room.

She paused, assuming this was the logical place to start, but Galvin asked, "*Is* there anything more to see in here?" and she realized that, of course, this room was so logical a place to start that Galvin must have already thoroughly searched it, and no doubt Brinna had either seen or been aware of him doing so.

Putting the blame on him, she answered, "*I* would have thought you were finished, but I'm just an ignorant serving maid."

He said, "You were in the kitchen when you heard Master Innis cry out…"

She nodded and led him back down the hall into the kitchen.

Galvin indicated for her to sit down.

So much for "Show me about the house," Nola thought.

She was worried that he would sit closely next to her, but he remained standing—which, of course, made him tower over her. Well, then, it was to be serious questioning and not flirting. All in all, that was a relief.

"So," Galvin said, "Brinna. Is there anything you'd like to tell me?"

"Didn't I tell you everything before?" Nola asked, hoping to delay, hoping to learn something.

"Did you?" Galvin put his foot up on the bench next to her and leaned in, giving him the advantage of nearness to go with his previous advantage of height.

"Yes," Nola said. The table was already pressing into

her back, and she couldn't retreat any further. "I caught just the merest glimpse of the man, and I'm not—"

Galvin interrupted. "What are you afraid of?"

Nola shrugged to indicate she didn't know what he was talking about.

"We won't let harm come to you."

It was the way he included Sergeant Halig—or perhaps by "we" he meant Lord Pendaran—that finally satisfied her that his interest in her was to learn more about the killing. She nodded, for Brinna would acknowledge what he had said. *We won't let harm come to you.* He probably meant that they would protect her from the culprit if she incriminated someone. But in truth, he and Halig and Pendaran and people like them were the biggest threat to her and her mother.

"Start at the beginning."

Because she didn't know exactly what Brinna had seen, what she had said, Nola countered with, "I was born."

Finally he looked exasperated with her. "Had a bad morning at the market, did you?"

She smiled innocently.

"Couldn't find a thing to buy?"

Nola worked to keep her face blank. *Fool!* she called herself. Of course Halig would have noticed that she'd returned from shopping without anything, without even the basket she had left with. That would be what he had told Galvin, and now that they were here in the kitchen, Galvin could see for himself.

She said, "People kept crowding me and pushing me and wanting to know all about last night and asking me the same questions over and over, and I couldn't stand it anymore. I couldn't breathe." It was how she sometimes felt when she became convinced people suspected her of being a witch. "I panicked. I dropped my basket and ran home."

"All right," he said. *Did* he believe her? He had a tendency to say everything so mildly that she couldn't tell if he was thinking *The poor thing!* or *Liar!* She was more inclined to believe the first, but she told herself that was just foolish wishful thinking. And then he spoiled everything by asking, "Are you afraid of Alan?"

Alan? He was suspicious of *Alan?*

"Oh, for goodness' sake!" she blurted out in exasperation. Too many years of being afraid, of seeing justice gone awry, of having to hide because she was a witch while she saw dishonest folk get richer and richer—all this caught up with her. "That's just like someone in authority: arrogant, corrupt, a bully, and first chance you get, jumping to the wrong conclusion."

His eyes widened in surprise. A bit-too-innocent surprise, she thought, a moment before he spoke. "You *are* perceptive to see all that on such short acquaintance. I usually try to hide at least some of my worst qualities so people don't guess what I truly am till I've said at least five or six sentences."

Nola, she told herself, *if you don't force this man into being your enemy, you'll be luckier than you deserve.* By trying to hide her fear, she was being so surly she was forcing a confrontation. Still, she couldn't resist finishing, "And too clever for your own good."

"*Can* someone be too clever for his own good?"

Oh, yes, she could have said. But she estimated she had already said far too much. She was fortunate that so far he seemed more amused than annoyed. *That,* she could thank Brinna's good looks for. If a plain girl acted this way, he wouldn't have taken it. She looked down at her hands in her lap.

Galvin sighed. "You were in the kitchen...," he prompted.

She nodded. "Scrubbing the floor. Cleaning up after supper." She remembered the crock of beans she had seen. "I was preparing for the next day's supper."

"Alone?"

"Yes."

"And Alan was...?"

"At that point," she said, hoping not to contradict anything Alan or Brinna had said earlier, "I didn't know." Hurriedly she continued, "I heard..." Galvin had asked where she was when Innis had cried out. Was that a trap? Had Brinna told him she heard Innis, or was it the box crashing to the floor that had brought her running? Nola had to trust that the hints she gathered from him were true, or she would end up being so vague and evasive that he would start suspecting her. All in a rush she said, "I heard a cry, and Alan and I came running, and we got to the door, and opened it, and there was Master Innis lying on the floor, bleeding."

"Who arrived at the door first?"

"It happened so fast." She could see Galvin wasn't going to settle for that. She had half a chance of giving the same answer Brinna had this morning. "I think I did." *Alan?* she thought again. Why was he suspecting Alan? Because her answers kept shifting? She didn't want to cast suspicion on Alan, but she didn't want Galvin suspecting her, either. "I'm sorry I'm so confused. Everything happened so fast, and I was frightened. People in the market kept having me repeat everything, and then—by saying it over and over—I remembered some things I hadn't even realized I'd noticed before." Not likely, but possible. And where was all this going to leave the real Brinna when she came back?

And it was just as Nola thought this that she looked up and saw Brinna through the open shutter, carrying her marketing basket, coming through the courtyard toward the kitchen door.

✪ CHAPTER TEN

NOLA JUMPED TO her feet. "I must go back to the market," she cried, "before someone finds my basket and decides to keep it! Master Kirwyn will be so vexed with me."

Even while Galvin opened his mouth to explain, "I'm sorry, but I have a few more questions," he got his foot down from the bench and took a step back as though suspecting she was about to trample him on her way out. It was a nice thought, but she didn't dare go any farther: If she went past him and he turned to follow or even to watch, he would be able to see out the window as clearly as she could.

So, instead, she hurriedly turned the other way, to face the table.

He said, "This doesn't have to take long, and I can explain to Master Kirwyn—"

"Only, let me put this pot on the fire first so it can start to simmer and be ready by supper," she blurted all in a rush, talking over his objections, trusting once more that Brinna's good looks would let her get away with being a dithering fool. She hoped Galvin didn't know enough about running a household to be aware that any beans she started heating now would be a sodden mush by suppertime.

"Brinna," Galvin said, still sounding patient, "really, I must insist—"

Ignoring Galvin and his protests, she picked up the pot in which the beans had been soaking. Then she let it slip through her hands. It hit the edge of the table, flipped over, and sent beans and water flying all over the floor. And over Galvin's leg.

"Oh!" Nola cried. "How clumsy of me! I'm so sorry." She grabbed a cloth and went toward him, but he wisely stepped away before she could inflict more damage, which showed a quickness to learn on his part that Nola had to admire. Nor did he yell at her, but she tallied that as one more benefit she owed to Brinna's appearance rather than as any credit to Galvin.

"Stay here," he ordered her, quietly though firmly, as if recognizing that her clumsiness might be an attempt at a diversion.

"Yes," she said, in a tone meant to indicate she'd never suggested going anywhere else. "Just getting out of your way." She stepped toward the window so that if he looked up now, she would block most of the view. Brinna was within five strides of the door. There was no way Nola could ever get out of here without transforming in plain sight of either her or Galvin.

There was only one other choice that Nola could think of: Transform Brinna.

But then, of course, Brinna would explain that she was the real Brinna, no matter how she looked.

Except, again of course, that the story would sound mad—at least at first.

How could Nola ensure that everyone would immediately and steadfastly take Brinna's claims as a sign of lunacy, so that they wouldn't listen to her long enough to realize she made sense and knew things only the real Brinna would know?

Unless...

With a pang of guilt for being a treacherous friend and a faithless daughter, Nola whispered the words to make Brinna cease to look like herself. And she concentrated, very hard, on picturing her mother's form.

The kitchen door flew open and Brinna strode in, her face bearing the features of Nola's mother, her hair gray and wild and off in all directions, her hands blue-veined and spotted, her shoulders slightly stooped. As soon as Brinna saw Nola—as soon as she saw someone in her own home, wearing her own face—she stopped as though she'd found her feet suddenly rooted to the ground.

For Galvin's benefit, Nola tried to sound a balance between friendly and cautious. "Hello, Mary. What are you doing back here?"

"Who are you?" Brinna demanded. Her voice, bounded by the restraints of Nola's mother's appearance, came out thin and creaky. Of course she heard the difference. Her hands flew up to her mouth, but that made matters worse, for she could see her old woman's hands. She gasped. "Who are you?" she repeated, sounding truly frightened now. "What's happening?"

Nola was aware that Galvin had stopped trying to make his breeches presentable and that he was watching Brinna as she alternately touched her face and stared at her hands. He was ready, she guessed, to move quickly if this visitor gave any indication of being dangerous.

Miserably, hating what she was doing to someone who had shown her only kindness, Nola forced herself to say in a quizzical tone, "Mary?"

"I'm not Mary," Brinna said, her voice cracking so that it sounded querulous. "I'm Brinna. Who are you, and what have you done to me?"

Galvin asked Nola, "You know this woman?"

She was going to be the death of herself, Nola was sure of it. But somehow she managed to get her voice working. "She and her daughter came here the other day, seeking employment. It didn't work out." The last thing Nola wanted to do was bring up the business about foretelling Innis's death. "She's a very sweet woman but…" Nola touched her head. It was a gesture she often had seen people do in her mother's presence. But when she saw Brinna's horrified expression, she had to soften it, to pretend that she had just been adjusting her hair. But Brinna and Galvin both knew what she was doing.

"No!" Brinna cried. "Lord Galvin, we met and spoke this morning before I left for market."

Nola couldn't afford to give Brinna time to make an appeal to reason. So she asked Brinna, "Where's your daughter? Where's Nola? She should know better than to let you wander about on your own." And she spared a thought for wondering what reckless situation her true mother might have wandered into.

"I'm not Mary," Brinna cried, frustration putting a hint of hysteria into her voice that didn't hurt Nola's cause. "I'm Brinna. And you, even though you look like me, are not."

Galvin moved to put himself between Nola and Brinna. "Madam," he said gently, "why don't you sit down and we can try to sort this matter out—"

Brinna smacked the hand with which he tried to take her by the elbow. "Don't call me *madam*," she said, "and don't take that let's-talk-calmly-to-the-crazy-woman-and-maybe-she'll-leave-us-alone tone with me."

Actually, Nola thought he'd done a good job of not sounding condescending, such a good job that she felt a prickle of panic. *Not now,* she warned herself. Panic would eat away at her concentration, and if her concentration slipped, so would the spells that held herself and Brinna to these false appearances. So knowing what a cruel thing she was doing, she said firmly, "I am Brinna, you are Mary. Look." And she held up a silver plate so that Brinna could see her reflection.

Brinna screamed and covered her face and began to cry.

Footsteps came running down the hall.

Halig was first into the kitchen, closely followed by Alan, with Kirwyn lagging behind. If there was to be trouble, Kirwyn was obviously willing to leave it to others.

Just as Galvin had placed himself between the two women to protect Nola, Halig now stepped between Galvin and the weeping Brinna.

"Mary," Alan said. "Has something happened to Nola?"

Brinna pulled her marketing basket off her arm and flung it, spilling peaches and carrots, and narrowly missing his head. "I'm Brinna!" she shouted.

"All right," Alan agreed soothingly. "Brinna. Has something happened to Nola?"

By then Kirwyn was in the room, and he said, "Is that crazy old woman back?"

Brinna looked around as though searching for something to throw at *him*.

"Should I arrest her, sir?" Halig asked Galvin.

"No!" Nola cried. Besides the fact that that would be extremely cruel to poor Brinna, who had been kind with them and done nothing worse than return home at the wrong time, putting her in a cell would mean that she would be surrounded by people when Nola let the transforming spell drop. Already Nola couldn't think how she'd ever be able to fix this situation without everybody

98

involved knowing that witchcraft was at work. Her vehemence had obviously surprised Galvin, who was watching her appraisingly. She tried not to sound as though her life depended on it, and repeated, "No. Don't put her into prison. She's just a poor, confused old woman. She doesn't mean any harm. She doesn't *do* any harm."

Just when things were looking up—just when Galvin shook his head at Halig to agree that Brinna shouldn't be arrested—Kirwyn came in with his opinion. "No?" he said with a snort.

He looked about to elaborate when Nola said emphatically, "No." She planned to talk over the objection he made. She knew he was going to tell how the very day of the night Innis was killed, this same woman had pointed at the silversmith and shrieked, "Death!" But Nola was not used to talking back, and her mind had gone blank with fear. How could she have been so stupid not to have realized that, of course, Kirwyn or Alan would mention this? She couldn't think over the thudding of her heart. Frantically she searched for something, and in the interim she realized that, for whatever reason, Kirwyn had obeyed her stern look and had stopped talking.

So she spoke instead to Brinna. "Please think calmly before you get yourself into trouble." It was good advice for herself, too. "You can only hurt yourself by persisting in this delusion. Do you want to end up in prison?" For Halig certainly still looked ready to carry out this threat.

Brinna had stopped crying. She was probably still

afraid, but now she was mostly angry. "You're behind this. You switched bodies with me."

Obviously she assumed Nola was Nola's mother. The fact that she was wrong about *that* wouldn't prevent her from saying the one thing Nola least wanted said out loud; she was about to use that dreaded word, "witchcraft."

So Nola once more pictured her mother. With all her concentration—using much more energy than she needed to change someone's form—she pictured her mother cradling her arm, humming a lullaby to the baby in her forefinger.

Brinna hugged herself as though she was cold or distressed. She opened her mouth to accuse Nola of witchcraft. No words came out, only a hum. Slowly she began to rock from side to side, cradling her arm. The hum became a snatch of melody. Nola could see the panic in her eyes. She could see Brinna trying to hold still, to let her arms drop to her sides, to stop humming.

Hating herself for what she was doing, Nola told Brinna, "I'm sure this fit won't last. It won't last long at all." This was all the comfort she dared offer, something she hoped the others would take as her simply humoring a crazy old woman. *It WON'T last long,* Nola assured herself. Just long enough to finish what needed doing here—which was to get downstairs without anybody noticing, disrupt the spell going on in the bucket, and be back at the market by noon so the farmer who had driven her into town would return her to the road to Saint Erim

Turi. What would happen after that—how she could possibly right things without admitting all to Brinna—she had no idea.

Brinna was fighting the spell, fighting to get words out.

Nola pictured her mother on the step of the silversmith's house that first evening, when Innis had hired them because he would be getting married within the week.

"Congratulations," Brinna blurted out. Her hands fluttered to her mouth as though to push the word she had not meant to say back in. But, "Congratulations," she repeated, just as Nola's mother had, in the voice of one of the others who lived in her head. Brinna sucked in her lips and bit down on them. She couldn't help herself, and the word escaped yet again, in a third voice: "Congratulations." She began to cry again.

Nola felt like crying, too.

And in that moment of sympathy, Nola's concentration slipped. "You're all blind," Brinna told the others. "*Look* at me."

Once more Nola drew the mental picture of her mother rocking the baby, and Brinna resumed humming, although it was obvious she didn't want to.

Galvin picked up the marketing basket she had flung. Did he recognize it as the one with which Brinna had left the house earlier? *Probably not,* Nola reassured herself. Men didn't notice things like baskets. In any case, he put the spilled items back in, then held it out to Brinna. She snatched it out of his hand before turning and stamping her feet every step of the way out the door, angry and frustrated and frightened all at once.

Though wishes by themselves accomplished nothing, *Stay safe,* Nola wished after her, by which she meant, among other things, *Don't do anything to get me in worse trouble.*

To herself, she asked, *What have you done? Gotten everyone looking suspiciously at your mother. THAT was very clever. A few more plans like that, and they'll burn you both at the stake.*

Alan said to Lord Pendaran's men, "She's harmless. Truly. I had an old aunt whose wits wandered for years, but she never caused hurt to any and—"

"Alan," Kirwyn interrupted, "nobody is interested in you or your various aunties, uncles, or half-witted cousins."

Alan immediately stopped talking and looked at his feet, instead.

Galvin gazed at Kirwyn with one of his unreadable expressions. To Alan he said, "I understand." To Nola, "You were showing me around the house."

He doesn't like Kirwyn any better than I do, Nola thought gleefully, *and he has to work very hard not to let it show.* She *had* to like him, at least a little bit, for that. A moment later, what Galvin had said sank in: Show me around the house.

Finally. This was her chance. If he'd only said it and meant it *before* Brinna had returned.

Though, of course, then the real Brinna would have entered the kitchen while Nola was in the cellar, witlessly solving one trouble without realizing a worse one had just come up behind her.

Could anything else go wrong now? Silly question. If life had taught her nothing else, it was that things could always get worse.

Galvin must have thought she was hesitating over worry for the spilled pot of beans, for he said, "I must insist that you set aside all else—"

"I recommend a systematic search," Nola interrupted. *Move fast,* every instinct warned her, *BEFORE the next catastrophe hits.* "From the bottom up, starting with the root cellar. From back to front."

Galvin nodded, looking amused at her sudden burst of efficiency.

Nola lit a candle from the fire in the hearth. "Careful," she warned. "The stairs are sturdy but steep."

"Perhaps I'd better—"

But she'd intentionally opened the door so that he had to step back, and by then she was on the narrow staircase and he had no choice but to follow.

Nola held her skirt up out of the way. The circle of light from the candle's flame showed the stairs, showed a crescent of the dirt of the root cellar's floor. From here she could not see the corner in which she'd placed the bucket and covered it with an old cloth. That was behind the stairs, only visible going up, not down. All she needed was to get there one step ahead of him, just enough time to kick rag and bucket over, to send shadowforms spilling into the darkness.

"Careful." Now it was Galvin warning her. "No need to go so fast—" Just as she took another step and put her foot down on the trailing edge of her skirt.

She threw her arms wide to grab the wall but felt only air. And then she pitched forward, head over heels, tumbling down the stairs, which smacked against her hands and knees, and then her back, and then there was a breathless moment of nothingness and she knew she'd rolled right off the edge of the stairs. And then she landed, flat on her back in the dark.

Clumsy fool! But at least she was in the dark, which meant the candle had gone out as she dropped it so she hadn't set herself on fire.

More important it meant nobody could see that—as well as knocking the breath out of herself—she had knocked the glamour out. She no longer looked like Brinna, but had resumed her true appearance. And wherever Brinna was, she once more looked like herself.

"Halig!" she heard Galvin cry. He didn't wait for the sergeant to fetch a fresh candle, but continued down the stairs, which was foolhardy without a light. How likely was he to make it down without tripping also and landing on top of her?

She managed to get in enough air to hastily whisper the words that made her once more take on the form of Brinna, and made Brinna—Nola fervently hoped she wasn't someplace public during all this shifting of appearances—resume the form of Nola's mother.

Galvin turned out not to be as ungainly as she, for the next moment he was beside her. "Brinna," he said, sounding simultaneously gentle and urgent. He knelt beside her, telling her, "Lie still."

"I feel a perfect fool," she mumbled. She could barely make out the rag-draped bucket, just far enough away that she couldn't reach it.

"Are you hurt anywhere?"

"I'm hurt *every*where."

"Well," Galvin said, "yes, I can imagine. But anywhere more than the rest?"

Nola could hear Halig coming down the stairs, and the cellar grew brighter from the candle he carried.

"Did any pieces of me detach on the way down?" she asked.

"If so, only very small pieces," Galvin assured her. "Did you hit your head?"

"I don't think so." But she couldn't be sure. She definitely felt light-headed. And thinking about her head was a mistake. Brain and stomach finally caught up with each other, and she realized she was going to vomit. Luckily Galvin realized it also. Somehow he got her on her side and supported her head while she heaved out the morning's meal not a handspan from his knee.

Halig, leaning over her, said, "That leg doesn't look good."

For a moment she feared he meant that her concentration had once again slipped, that the transforming spell had wavered and she had ceased to look like Brinna and had once more taken on her true form. But surely they would have reacted much more strongly if her entire appearance had changed. She tried to sit up, and Galvin pushed her back down.

He touched her ankle and she gasped at the pain. She smacked him as hard as she could, which she knew wasn't showing proper appreciation for his not letting her choke on her own vomit, but in any case it wasn't enough to make him let go.

Alan, standing at the top of the stairs with Kirwyn, called down, "Is it broken?"

"Difficult to say," Galvin answered.

"It's only sprained," Nola answered, hoping. "I'm all right. Truly. Let me up."

Galvin looked skeptical, but he helped her sit.

Her back ached, and her knees and shins and palms were sore, and her right foot definitely drooped at the end of her leg. "Just a sprain," she repeated, less sure now, but desperate to get up long enough to reach that bucket.

"Don't—," Galvin started as she struggled to get to her feet, but she swatted his hands away and leaned instead on Halig, who if he didn't look confident in her, at least seemed willing to let her try.

She fought a wave of dizzy nausea, telling herself that her stomach was empty anyway. "There." She stood with her weight on her left foot, clinging to Halig, knowing that she would not be able to take even one step on that right foot. But she had maneuvered herself and the sergeant a couple steps closer to the bespelled bucket of water.

Be strong, she admonished herself. While the spell for shadowforms would last as long as hair and bespelled water remained undisturbed, transforming spells lasted only while she concentrated. If she passed out, the spells that made her look like Brinna, and Brinna look like her mother, would dissolve. And yet she knew this was going to hurt like anything.

Since her right ankle would be unable to support her weight, she had to stand on her left foot. So she had only her injured right leg to work with. She took a steadying breath and a strong hold on her glamour, then—as though she fully·planned to walk up those stairs—she swung her leg so that it smacked against the bucket. Colored lights exploded in the corners of her eyes, but she didn't faint.

Galvin swore, but it wasn't for seeing the shadowforms revealed. It was because she'd successfully upended the bucket and had—once again—soaked his leg in the process. But the bucket was upside down; that was the important thing. The spell that had been eavesdropping on the man with the blackberry field in Low Beck had ended.

"Sorry," she said, relief and pain and weakness conspiring to make her barely able to mumble the word. She became aware that it was only Halig's strong arm that had kept her from collapsing.

"Here…," Galvin said, and the next moment he'd picked her up and was climbing the stairs, which was so absurd it was embarrassing.

"Put me down," she protested.

"It's the only way *I'll* feel safe," Galvin told her. He carried her to Brinna's room and set her down gently on the bed. "Do you have anything to bind that ankle with?" he asked.

Alan went scurrying to get some cloths, while Kirwyn shook his head and complained, "If it isn't one thing, it's another."

"I'm sorry," Nola told him, told all of them for the trouble she was causing. But she'd be out of their lives soon.

"Broken or sprained," Galvin said, "you're going to have to stay off that foot for a while."

"A while?" Nola squealed. She was thinking of the farmer who had offered her a ride—*if* she was back at the market by noon. She was thinking of Brinna, looking like her mother. She was thinking of her mother, up to who-knew-what mischief. Nola tried to swing her legs off the bed, but Galvin pushed her back. She caught a glimpse of her ankle, which was swelling already. By concentrating on what a normal leg looked like, she could make her ankle appear neither bruised nor swollen, but that would do nothing for the pain. "I have things to do," she protested.

"What?" Galvin asked.

Since she couldn't very well say, "Go back to my mother before she gets herself into trouble," or "Leave before everyone realizes I'm a witch," she said the only thing she could think of: "Get the house ready for Sulis, who was to marry Innis and who doesn't know any of this and is on her way here."

In the voice of one who is reminding rather than informing, Galvin said, "Kirwyn sent word this morning and told her not to come. You were standing right there when he said so."

Nola licked her lips. "Maybe." For an excuse she added, "Sometimes I don't listen."

Galvin glanced back at Kirwyn still hovering in the doorway. Then he looked back at her and said, not quite straight-faced, "Yes," for which Nola liked him a little better.

But she still didn't forgive him for carrying her up the stairs.

✿ CHAPTER ELEVEN

Sᴇʀɢᴇᴀɴᴛ Hᴀʟɪɢ ʙᴏᴜɴᴅ Nola's ankle in cloths soaked in cool rose water. It relieved some of the pain, but an icy stream would have felt even better. Nola remembered the stream by which she had stopped last night, the one near which the farmer had picked her up this morning and to which he had promised to return her—*if* she was waiting for him in the market by noon.

If it wasn't noon yet, it was certainly close. Too close for a lame witch who had miscalculated her own cleverness and luck.

It could be worse, she told herself.

But she would have to concentrate to think *how,* and she needed to spend her concentration on maintaining her spells.

Nobody had seen the shadowforms in the bucket, she reminded herself. Only Brinna knew she was a witch, and—for the moment—Brinna had no proof of this and no likelihood that anyone would believe whatever she had to say. Not that Nola could let herself relax. She was trapped in a house with four men, none of whom was likely to be any help to her at all: two who, should they begin to suspect she was a witch, had the authority to arrest her; one who was desperate enough to have just killed his father; and one who looked about to get blamed for that killing. *It could be worse,* Nola mentally repeated: Halig could be binding her to a stake rather than nursing her swollen ankle, or Kirwyn could be standing in the doorway with a hatchet and a crazed look on his face rather than with the cup of water and bowl Galvin had sent him to fetch and the put-upon expression of one who was used to doing the ordering rather than the fetching. Alan was supposed to be helping Halig, but he was so agitated he seemed to be doing more fluttering than helping.

Galvin took the cup and bowl from Kirwyn and brought them to Nola, which increased the sourness on Kirwyn's face. As Galvin supported her so that she could rinse the taste of vomit from her mouth, Nola couldn't help but smile.

Galvin, of course, caught her at it. "What?" he asked.

Nola shook her head. "An old family story," she explained. "Apparently my mother would get sick every morning while she was carrying me, before I was born. She likes to tell how my father would stroke her hair and sing songs to comfort her. It's one of her sayings: Never underestimate someone who's willing to hold your head while you're being sick."

"Ah, well," Galvin said. He took the bowl she'd used

to spit in but left her the cup, which still held water. "I don't sing."

"My mother never said my father sang *well*," Nola pointed out.

"Your mother sounds like a very sensible woman."

So much for any thought of intelligent conversation with him.

"I'd feel much better if I could just rest quietly," Nola told everyone, though in truth she wanted them out of there precisely so that she could sit up and pinch herself if she started to get sleepy. With the ache in her ankle a dull throb, she might too easily drift off, and that would be the end of the transforming spell that held her in this form and Brinna in her mother's.

"Rest is the best medicine," Halig agreed.

As the sergeant ushered them out of the room, Galvin said, "So, Alan. Fetch a candle and Halig and I can take a quick look at the root cellar."

Just in time. She'd gotten to the bucket just in time.

"The root cellar?" Kirwyn had stopped moving. "You've already been down there. Surely you remember? Dark room at the foot of the stairs? Brinna tumbling down, you and the sergeant running after, her emptying her stomach practically all over you...?"

Galvin ignored the sarcasm. "We went down there," he said. "We didn't look."

Kirwyn gave a loud sigh.

"Strictly a precaution," Galvin told him. "With Brinna screaming when she discovered your father's body, and you and Alan yelling as you pursued the intruder, the neighbors were alerted very quickly. And yet with all those people opening their doors and hanging out their windows, *nobody* saw anyone run out of your courtyard." Galvin gave a frosty smile. "Only you and Brinna saw any glimpse of an intruder."

"He was fast," Kirwyn protested.

Kirwyn claimed to have seen the intruder, too? No wonder Galvin was so suspicious; their descriptions probably didn't match.

"Or," Galvin said, "he may have circled around the back and reentered the house through the kitchen door."

This had gone too far for Nola to continue feigning sleepiness. "Why?" she demanded.

"To hide until the commotion moved to the other end of the house. Then, once everyone had given up on pursuit and was gathered around the shop, he could have strolled out the kitchen door without anyone noticing."

Galvin is definitely too clever for his own good, Nola thought. He was complicating things even more than she had. Did he really believe this far-fetched theory, or was he trying to catch someone up? And if he was trying to catch someone up, who? She asked, "So that would mean that you're searching for…?"

Galvin made an expansive gesture. "Evidence of his being here. Or perhaps he left the stolen goods hidden somewhere in the house, with the plan of coming back to retrieve them at some later time, when things have calmed. Which, of course, would put all of you in danger. He might even still be here, trapped by the searchers coming back sooner than he anticipated. For all we know, he's in a corner of the root cellar, or in or behind a piece of furniture."

Nola glanced at Halig to see what he made of that notion but couldn't read anything from his face.

If Galvin said too much more, she would have to throw something out of sheer vexation. So Nola closed her eyes to indicate that she was tired and that they should leave.

When she peeked her eyes open, she saw that Galvin, Halig, and Alan had gone, and only Kirwyn remained, lingering in the doorway. She remembered how he'd looked when she'd seen him in the bespelled water before he had killed Innis. He'd been spying in the kitchen window, watching Brinna, and he'd been wearing an expression of venom and malice. Now his expression was only one of irritation. "What the hell are you trying to do, Brinna?" he demanded in a quiet voice, obviously intent on not letting the others hear.

Trying to do? "I fell," she told him.

He continued to glower.

Pain and the weariness of habitual fear conspired to make her reckless. "I didn't fall intentionally to inconvenience you."

Surprisingly he didn't take offense at her unservant-like brazenness. "Is anything amiss?" he asked.

Everything was. Everything obviously was. Even Kirwyn had to see that. And solicitude didn't suit him. Even his tone of voice was wrong. "No," she said, though she was not sure what exactly he was asking her.

"Good," he snapped.

"Thank you for your concern," she muttered as he slammed the door shut.

What was *that* all about?

He would bear watching.

But of course she had known *that* already.

She waited until the men's voices and their footsteps faded, then she reached for the cup Galvin had left her. Since this was Brinna's bed, she had no difficulty finding one of Brinna's hairs. Whispering the words that prepared the water, she tossed the hair into the cup.

The magic was not fooled by the transforming spell. Instantly Brinna's shadowform appeared in the water. Looking like Nola's mother, she sat, huddled and miserable, in the corner of what appeared to be a barn. *Good*, Nola thought, happy not over Brinna's distress but because Brinna was being quiet. And because she was alone. That was safest for both of them. And she had the basket she'd taken marketing, which meant she wouldn't go hungry, even if Nola couldn't get out of the house until after everyone had gone to bed.

But Nola hoped she'd have a chance before that. She hoped that Innis was to be buried today—it was, after all, summer—and that she could slip away then.

Lest Brinna get the idea that she was safe just because

she was away from Nola's presence, Nola concentrated on the memory of her mother trying to snatch fairies only she could see out of the air. "Damn fairies," her mother would say, "always jeering and poking fun."

In the cup, Brinna's hand jerked and clawed at the air and her lips twitched.

Nola made her do it only twice, just so she wouldn't dare to go to her friends to try to convince them of what had happened. Then Nola plucked the hair out of the cup. There were more to choose from should she decide to check again, and she would never, ever, leave bespelled water about again. She was determined not to complicate the situation any more than she already had.

Galvin was doing enough of that already.

✥

ALAN BROUGHT HER a meal, proof—if she'd needed any—that she'd lost any possibility of returning to the farmer's market stall in time for him to return her to the road to Saint Erim Turi.

"What's happening?" Nola asked.

"Much coming and going," Alan replied. "Lord Pendaran's men searched the house, the shop, and the grounds. They've questioned neighbors." Alan shrugged, possibly indicating he considered much of this a waste of time—which it would have been had Innis really been killed by an intruder.

"And Kirwyn?" Nola asked.

"Accepting the condolences of all…as well as accepting a few work orders." No need of brilliant deduction to guess what Alan thought of *that* unseemly haste to return to business.

Trying to get more information, Nola said, "That Lord Galvin, he makes my head spin."

"Well, yes," Alan said, "he does seem to have that effect on quite a few of the young women."

"No." Nola felt her face go red. "I mean with all his theories, all his questions." She was sure Alan didn't believe her. *Serves you right,* she told herself, *after making it so no one believes Brinna.* She went on, "He got me so muddled, I couldn't remember what I'd told him before. I couldn't remember what I'd *seen* before."

Alan patted her hand sympathetically. "And the knock on your head won't be helping any."

"Exactly," Nola agreed. She didn't need sympathy; she needed to know what had happened last night after she stopped watching in the bespelled water basin. "I remember being in the kitchen when I heard Master Innis cry out." She paused and hugged herself as though too distressed to continue, in case Alan would correct her and say that previously she had claimed it was the thud of the strongbox falling that had alerted her that something was wrong.

Alan didn't correct her.

"And I remember running down the hallway, where you joined me because you were coming from…" She reached for her cup and took a drink of water.

"My room," Alan finished for her, which was some of the information she'd been hoping to uncover.

She nodded, pretending he was saying something she already knew. "Then," she continued—Alan had already indicated this in front of Galvin—"I opened the door—"

Alan interrupted with another detail. "Because I was slower, being already asleep when the cry awoke me…"

Again Nola nodded. "And I saw…I *think* I saw…a glimpse of him. The one who did it."

Alan didn't say anything, because apparently Brinna had said no such thing last night.

"I shouldn't have said anything to Galvin," Nola said, "because I'm not sure. Maybe people talked me into it, with all their questions." She tested out that explanation, and Alan seemed to find it reasonable, but that was no assurance Galvin had.

"Maybe you saw his shadow," Alan said, a compromise between "I saw him" and "I didn't see him."

"Maybe," Nola agreed. "But, you know, after that everything seems confused."

"Everything *was* confused after that." Alan was just too agreeable. But then he continued, "Neighbors shouting and pursuing each other, everybody with opinions and advice, the baker's wife coming to help and then fainting…"

Galvin had mentioned something about Brinna screaming and Kirwyn and Alan pursuing. Nola said, "So while I was busy screaming, you and Kirwyn went chasing after the intruder…"

"See, you do remember," Alan said.

"And…What direction, again, did Kirwyn come from? Was he behind you in the hall?" That would have made sense if Kirwyn had run out of the shop and circled around the house, entering through the kitchen so that he, too, could say that he had been asleep in his own room. This would have given him the opportunity to throw the money he had stolen from his father's strongbox into his room, to hide more carefully later.

But where *had* he hidden it, if Galvin and Halig had searched the house and been unable to find it?

None of this made any difference, for Alan was shaking his head. "No, Kirwyn came around from the outside, thinking to cut him off."

That meant he must have dropped or quickly stowed the stolen money outside. And yet none of the neighbors who had swarmed into the courtyard to see what was happening last night had come across it. Nor had Galvin and Halig today. And what chance had Kirwyn had to remove it to a safer place? Nola tried to picture the outside of the house, the courtyard. Surely Galvin and Halig would have had the sense to look into the well. And to check both the well and the outside of the house for loose stones behind which a treasure could be hidden. It couldn't have been a very complicated hiding place, because there was so little time for Kirwyn both to have scooped the money out of the strongbox *and* to have hidden it.…

Leave that hunt to the men, Nola told herself.

And yet maybe it was important. Maybe *where* the money was hidden could in some way point Galvin and Halig to *who* had hidden it. Though she couldn't help but wonder *why* Kirwyn had stolen at all—when in the end, as Innis's only son, Kirwyn would get everything anyway.

With that thought, Nola suddenly saw the *why*—not of the robbery, but of the murder itself. Innis was about to remarry. If he died after that, Kirwyn's inheritance would have to be shared with the new bride, Sulis. And if in the course of time Innis and Sulis had children, especially a boy, especially since Innis and Kirwyn didn't get along…

"You're thinking very hard," Alan told her.

Nola smiled and reminded herself not to concentrate all of her attention on Kirwyn or she'd be in danger of accidentally letting slip the transforming spell that held her to Brinna's appearance. It was not up to her to solve the hows and whys of the silversmith's murder. That was Galvin and Halig's responsibility. What she needed was to learn enough about what had happened that she could trick Galvin into believing she had been there—trick him long enough for her to find an opportunity to get out of the house, out of Haymarket, and back to her mother— Lord! There was a thought!—waiting for her in Saint Erim Turi. If Halig and Galvin couldn't figure out the *who* of this matter—or worse yet, settled on Alan—that was unfortunate, but it didn't, really, affect her.

It didn't, she mentally repeated.

Not that the repetition made it more convincing.

Out loud she said to Alan, "Just trying to get everything resettled in my mind, before Galvin comes in and confuses me all over again."

"Well," Alan said, "eat your lunch. Things always look better on a full stomach. And I need to see if Kirwyn needs help in the shop, before he comes looking for me."

"Thank you for preparing the meal," Nola said. "I'm sorry to be laid up and put more work on you."

"Not your fault," Alan assured her. "And Master Kirwyn has hired the cooper's daughters to prepare the funeral feast this afternoon."

Nola was glad to hear that Kirwyn didn't expect her to get up and hobble around the kitchen, but Alan seemed to be waiting for a reaction from her. "Well," she said, "good."

"No comment?" Alan asked, with a grin that indicated Brinna had strong opinions regarding the cooper's daughters.

Having no idea what those opinions could be, Nola asked, "Such as...?"

"*Such as* that there never were two such lazy girls," Alan said. "They're too lazy to shoo flies off themselves."

"That goes without saying," Nola answered. "Let's hope there will be no flies this afternoon."

As he was stepping out the door, Nola called after him, just to be sure, one more question. "And last night, was Kirwyn in his room also?"

Alan looked at her blankly.

"When Master Innis was attacked and we heard him shout?"

"He was in the kitchen," Alan said. "With you."

Nola hastily took a drink to hide her surprise. Brinna couldn't have provided Alan with that information because Brinna would have known Kirwyn wasn't there. But maybe Brinna hadn't heard this claim yet. Nola asked, "Is that what he said?"

"That's what both of you said."

"Both of us?" Kirwyn had killed Innis. Nola had seen that. Brinna had been alone in the kitchen; Kirwyn had peeked in on her for a few moments, and then he had gone around to the shop and killed Innis. Nola had seen this with her own eyes.

Alan was laughing at her. "Eat, and then rest," he said. "It's one thing for Lord Galvin to make your head spin. It's a sad moment when *I* can send you into a muddle."

To indicate she would take his advice, Nola smiled, though it probably wasn't much of a smile.

"It was a terrible and confusing time for all of us," Alan offered, just before closing the door behind him.

Terrible and confusing for Brinna, Nola thought. Obviously Kirwyn had been in the kitchen with her just before Nola had used the bespelled water to look in on them. He had left just as Nola was casting the spell and so she had been just in time to see him look in the window, then he had gone and killed Innis, and Brinna—in

122

the horror of finding Innis murdered and in the pande-
monium that followed—had forgotten that Kirwyn
wasn't with her all along.

There couldn't be any other explanation.

Could there?

✡ CHAPTER TWELVE

Why in the world would Brinna lie to protect Kirwyn?

Surely, Nola thought, after backing away from the thought and having to circle back around to it, *surely Brinna has more sense than to be in love with him*.

Nola had to believe *anyone* would have more sense than to be in love with Kirwyn.

She remembered once again the expression she had witnessed on his face, when he hadn't realized anyone was watching him watch Brinna—when Nola had first realized, even before she saw him kill his father, that he was dangerous. But she also remembered the night before, the one night she and her mother had spent under the silversmith's roof, seeing Kirwyn's clumsy attempt to put his arm around Brinna's waist. Brinna had deftly eluded him, which certainly seemed proof she didn't want him.

But maybe, Nola thought, even if Brinna didn't love him, she felt sorry for him.

No, that was ridiculous. *You don't lie to protect a murderer simply because you feel sorry that he loves you and you don't love him back,* Nola reasoned. Especially if you were someone like Brinna. Brinna was used to people loving her. *Everybody* loved Brinna. Nola saw that with Galvin's reactions to her. And Halig's. And they'd only just met her.

More likely Kirwyn had threatened her, convinced her that he could cause her harm—some threat so strong that she would fear him even if he was arrested.

Or it might be that Brinna was simply mistaken. In the horror and chaos of Innis's murder, she had simply lost track of who was where.

But whether Brinna had lied or had been confused about Kirwyn being in the kitchen with her, Kirwyn had to be worrying that she might change her story. That made Brinna a threat to him.

Which made Kirwyn a threat to Nola.

People started arriving at the house, beginning with two young women who had to be the cooper's daughters. They came into Brinna's room—several times—chattering and giggling and asking where they could find this and that in the kitchen. Each time, Nola pretended that they had awakened her, hoping that they'd take her feigned grogginess as the reason why she didn't chat with them—rather than that she had no idea what their names were. Eventually they took pity and stopped plaguing her.

But others came then, neighbors and friends bearing

food—people whom Nola didn't know, whose relationships with Brinna she had no way of guessing. Many had no compunction about sticking their heads into the sickroom to offer their condolences and their advice, and she feared that they'd see through her act of ache and exhaustion. And it was becoming less and less an act. She had walked most of the previous day and half the night, and she wasn't used to lying in bed doing nothing.

It would be *so* easy to drift off.

Don't fall asleep, she mentally prodded herself. If the spell that made her look like Brinna slipped away while she dozed, that was sure to be the time one last person would decide to look in on the poor invalid.

Eventually the priest came, and the noise of the crowd moved down the hall. They were getting Innis's body for burial. Nola squeezed her eyes tight, trying not to imagine what Innis looked like under the burial shroud, trying not to imagine the sad face Kirwyn would be wearing for the benefit of all those onlookers.

The outer door shut behind the last of them, bringing blissful silence. Nola had to fight to get her eyes back open. It would be so wonderful to rest, truly rest, just for a moment, before she got up and started her long, long way back to Saint Erim Turi to unravel whatever catastrophe her mother had woven in her absence.

Someone knocked lightly on the bedroom door.

Nola gathered the transforming spell about herself like a shawl.

"Brinna?" It was Galvin's voice.

"Yes?" She struggled to sit up.

He opened the door. "Everyone has gone to the funeral," he said.

She nodded, relieved that she hadn't gotten up the moment she'd heard the guests leave. As soon as Galvin left, too...

He told her, "I will remain here. Just in case last night's intruder returns—or some other thief, taking the opportunity of an empty house."

"That's a fine idea," Nola managed to say, hoping he couldn't read her true thoughts on her face, her *GO, GO, GO, DAMMIT* thoughts.

He smiled kindly. "I'm sorry I disturbed you. But I was afraid you'd wake up and not hear anybody, and then you'd become worried for fear of being alone."

The worst part was she suspected he wasn't goading her as part of some convoluted plan to get the truth out of her, but that he was being entirely sincere.

"Can I get you something to eat?" he offered. "First choice of all that food laid out."

"No. Thank you."

Still he hesitated. She wondered if he was deciding whether to talk to her further about last night. The way things seemed to be going, she guessed that now that she had the answers he wouldn't ask any more questions. And, indeed, what he asked was, "Are you feeling better? Is there anything I can do to make you more comfortable?"

"I'm fine," she assured him. Sore, exhausted, frantic, and increasingly annoyed, but fine.

He didn't look convinced. Judging by how she felt, she probably looked too pale and weary for someone who had supposedly rested all afternoon—like someone in worse pain than she actually felt. That worked out to her advantage, for he nodded and stepped back into the hall. "I'll let you rest. Call out if you need anything."

"Yes. Thank you."

Nola sighed and tried to be patient. And to remain alert. Or at least awake. She had to hang on to both her glamour and her wits.

Galvin, too, she remembered, had traveled through the night. Maybe, alone in the kitchen and bored, if she was lucky, *he* would fall asleep.

She knew not to count on luck.

Better to count on simply going out through the bedroom window rather than one of the doors. She swung her legs over the edge of the bed but hesitated. For the moment, in its bindings, her ankle didn't feel too bad; but she knew that as soon as she stood, the increased blood flow would make it throb.

Though there was no sound from the kitchen, she had to fight the foreboding that somebody was about to burst in: Galvin, or the returning funeral guests—though that was unlikely, for they had left such a short time ago. But maybe the cooper's daughters would come back early to ask where Brinna kept the salt, or Alan, eager to fetch something he hoped would please her.

There's time, she assured herself. *Don't rush. The important thing is to be absolutely silent.*

She tightened the laces on her bodice then found her shoes, which someone—Sergeant Halig, she thought—had taken off when they'd put her to bed. She had trouble getting the right one on because of the swelling and bandages; and once it *was* on, she was unable to fasten it.

With one hand on the bed and one on the wall, she stood, holding her breath for fear of breathing too loudly. She tried putting just a little weight on the injured foot. It hurt, but not beyond enduring. She tried actually taking a step and had to clamp her teeth together to keep from crying out in pain.

You have to do this, she warned herself. *You have to get out of here.*

She was able to hobble forth a few steps, as long as she had something to hold on to: the bed, the clothes chest.

It took forever to cross the room, which, when she and her mother had stayed here, had seemed barely large enough to accommodate the two extra mattresses.

You don't have to get far, she reminded herself. Once she was outside, she could take on a different appearance and sit and gather her strength for as long as she needed.

So long as Galvin didn't pick now to look in on her.

Alan had thoughtfully closed the shutters in an attempt to make the room dark enough for sleeping. Nola tried to pull them open, but they simply rattled faintly.

Nola held her breath and listened with all her might.

The noise couldn't have been loud enough to have alerted Galvin in the next room.

Could it?

Sure that she had to move quickly to avoid being discovered, she tugged impatiently, and the tiny latch she hadn't seen was yanked out of the wood.

The shutters swung open, one flying free of her grip and slamming against the wall, while the other came back at her face so that she instinctively stepped back. Her ankle gave out under her, and she sat down, fast and heavy.

Galvin burst in.

While it had taken her so long and so many mincing steps to get from bed to window, he was across the room in a few quick strides, just long enough to draw his sword from its sheath with a metallic scrape that she was sure would be the last thing she heard. She'd never before seen a sword blade so close, and glinting in the late-afternoon sunlight it was much longer, much sharper-looking than she'd have guessed. Obviously he'd determined she was a witch and took her trying to escape as proof. She flinched and braced herself and hoped that her mother would be able to get along on her own.

Instead of swinging the sword, Galvin demanded, "What happened? Did someone try to get in?"

She opened her eyes and saw that he had one foot up on the window frame, ready to leap out into the yard, ready to take off in pursuit, except that he couldn't see anyone to pursue.

"Are you hurt?" Galvin asked, with his attention still on surveying the yard.

"No," Nola said, only now beginning to breathe again. "*I* opened the window." That needed an excuse so that it wouldn't sound like the escape attempt it was. "I was hot and needed some air."

"Did you hear anything?" Galvin persisted. "Did a noise awaken you?"

"I was hot," Nola repeated, finally beginning to believe that he wasn't going to execute her for witchcraft after all. "There was no one out there. I forgot about the latch and broke it."

Finally Galvin looked at her. "Sorry," he said, and she could read the sheepishness in his voice and in his expression and in the way his shoulders slumped and he seemed to get smaller—like a cat calming down after a fright. He was embarrassed for reacting too strongly, for running in here to protect her from a danger that didn't exist.

He set the blade back in its sheath, then crouched beside her. He laid his hand gingerly on her bandaged ankle, as though half expecting that her foot might come off in his hand.

"It just went out from under me," Nola assured him. "I didn't twist it."

He shook his head. "If you needed the window opened, you should have called me."

She said, "I didn't want to disturb you."

It was a ridiculous excuse, and it did nothing to explain why she had needed to put on her shoes.

He didn't mention that. He had started out concerned, then become embarrassed, and now he looked to be moving fast toward annoyance. His voice sounding considerably more patient than she would have guessed from his face, he asked, "Are you hurt?"

"No," she told him. "Well, no more than I was to begin with, after my flight off the stairs."

He shook his head again, but his pique seemed to be melting into exasperation.

Brinna, she reminded herself. Any special consideration was because she looked like Brinna.

He stood and made a show of opening the shutters, then securing them. "Can you stand?" he asked.

Since the alternative was for him to carry her, she nodded.

He moved between her and the wall and hoisted her under her arms. She saw that the reasonable thing for her to do was to place her arm over his shoulder to support her weight, and it was only by happy coincidence that this put her hand close to his hair.

Though she had no specific plan, she intentionally caught her finger around a single strand, then she slipped down a bit as though too weary to stand upright. He must have assumed that she tugged accidentally, and he neither flinched nor yelped. She closed her fist around the captured hair and, with Galvin's help, was able to hobble back to the bed.

He picked up her legs and swung them onto the mattress. Without a word he took her shoes off, being gentle with the wedged-on right one, and placed them back beside the bed.

Then he sat down on the edge of the bed. "Since you apparently can't sleep anyway," he said, "perhaps we might talk a little more about what happened last night."

She guessed she wouldn't get very far claiming to feel faint, so she didn't try. "What did you want to know?"

"The same that I've been asking all along." His voice was quiet, patient, but intense.

Nola sighed as though weary of telling the same story over and over. "I was in the kitchen," she said, "cleaning up after supper, preparing for the next day. Alan..." She remembered that this morning she had claimed she didn't know where Alan was. "I...wasn't sure where Alan was...*at that time*, while I was in the kitchen." She made sure to emphasize that, for she certainly didn't want Alan to get blamed for Kirwyn's crime because of *her* statements. "He'd said he was tired, but I hadn't actually seen him go into his room—it's that cubbyhole by the stairs—though when I was running down the hallway, after Master Innis cried out...directly after he cried out"—she didn't want Galvin thinking Alan had had time to circle back—"I heard the door to his room open, and Alan came running out practically on my heels."

Galvin was looking at her with that infuriating mild, appraising expression, and she realized she was saying too much, covering everything too well in one rush of details that was not characteristic of the way a normal person talked, certainly not characteristic of the vague and elusive way she had talked previously. Despite all its stops and reversals, her speech sounded—even to her ears—rehearsed.

"I've been thinking about our conversation this morning," she explained, "and realized—the way I left it—that you might have gotten the wrong impression."

And that explanation didn't help one bit, she saw.

She closed her eyes, not to be distracted by him, then realized that might give the wrong impression, too, and opened them. She licked her dry lips. *Just go on.* "We ran down the hall. I opened the door. I saw Master Innis lying on the floor, his silver scattered about him. I may or may not have seen something in the far doorway. Maybe it was just a shadow. I don't know. It was dark and I was frightened."

"Are you frightened now?"

"No," she said, assuming he meant was she afraid of him. Then, "Yes," she amended, in case he meant was she afraid of the murderer coming back, which Brinna might be. Then, "No," she settled on, remembering he had previously asked whether she was afraid of Alan.

There was no sign of the hint of a smile he customarily wore for her. *For Brinna,* she reminded herself. "Where was Kirwyn?" he asked coldly.

Kirwyn. What should she say about Kirwyn? *In the kitchen* would exonerate him. *I don't know* would open her up to suspicion for changing Brinna's story.

In the face of her hesitation, Galvin asked testily, "Do

you need me to refresh your memory? When I first spoke with you, you said he'd been in the kitchen with you. After you came back from the market, you said you were alone in the kitchen. Now is your chance to change that answer again, if you want: You were in the kitchen, surrounded by a troupe of singing monks, perhaps?"

Nola held on to a mental picture of Brinna, lest the image before Galvin start quivering like a reflection in a bowl of water that's been jostled. She hoped Brinna was alone, for she had nothing to spare for maintaining Brinna in her mother's form. Nor had she anything left for answering Galvin's sarcasm.

"What happened in the market?" Galvin asked.

"Nothing," Nola said.

"Why did your story change after you came back?"

"It didn't." *Don't cry,* Nola told herself, though she was so exhausted and frightened she felt close to it. Galvin would not be moved by tears.

"Either Kirwyn was with you or he was not."

"What I meant," Nola said, "was that I was in the kitchen, scrubbing the floor. Kirwyn *was* with me, the last time I'd looked. But—" She had to stop licking her lips; she knew it made her look like the guilty liar she was, but she couldn't help herself: Her mouth was so dry. "I had my back to the door, and he was behind me. So, you see, I didn't exactly see him, so I felt alone. Though I wasn't. Because Kirwyn was there, too."

Galvin just sat looking at her.

And she sat holding on to the edges of her glamour, which felt ready to fly off like a floppy hat on a windy day.

He has kind eyes, Nola remembered Brinna saying in answer to someone's comment that Galvin had pretty eyes. They *were* an attractive gray, but cold. There was no kindness in them now. Everything in his expression called her a liar. She fought not to flinch, not to glance away guiltily.

"Did Kirwyn kill Innis?" Galvin asked.

The question took Nola's breath away. "Kirwyn?" she asked on half a sigh. He suspected Kirwyn after all? Despite all his questions about Alan? About an intruder? She saw he was studying her, catching the relief that must have flickered across her face. And what did he make of that? "I wasn't there when Innis died," was all she dared say. "I was in the kitchen."

Galvin's voice became more gentle, though his eyes were no warmer. "Did Kirwyn have reason to want his father dead?"

Yes! she wanted to shout. *You're finally asking the right questions.* But she couldn't get her voice above a whisper. "They argued frequently. He wouldn't have liked to share an inheritance with the new wife." Surely some of the neighbors would have told him this earlier. "But if it was Kirwyn, why would he steal the money? It could only be a danger, slowing him down, proving he was the culprit if it was found on him. Why risk that when it was part of his inheritance?"

Galvin hesitated, though Nola suspected he had worked out an answer already and was simply weighing whether to share it with her. "To make the killing appear to be done by someone else," he suggested.

Nola was aware that her mouth formed a silent "Oh." She felt like a naive child. Not that she had ever been a naive child, or at least not in a very long time.

Galvin was watching her closely. "What about Alan? Did he have reason to hate his master?"

Nola closed her eyes in frustration.

There was a rattle from the gate that led into the courtyard.

Brinna! Nola thought. In her panic about Galvin's questions, she had forgotten to concentrate on keeping her mother's form on Brinna, and now Brinna was back to accuse and offer proof—

The kitchen door opened, and the sound of many voices came into the house. The funeral party was returning.

Nola mentally pictured her mother's form overlapping Brinna's.

In the meantime, Galvin's attention never wavered. He had to have seen the dread on her face and how it was replaced by relief. He spoke slowly and calmly, though they had only a few more moments. "If you were Kirwyn, and you had killed your father and stolen his money to make it look like the work of an intruder, what would you do with the money?"

"I don't know," Nola said. Which was the truth,

but Galvin had no way of knowing that after all her lies.

And then people were stopping in front of the open door, looking in at her on the bed and Galvin sitting there beside her.

Kirwyn smirked, raising his eyebrows suggestively. "My, my, did we come back too soon?"

"Yes," Galvin said. He stood, ignoring the knowing grins on most of the faces of those crowded around Kirwyn.

Kirwyn glowered. It was the look he had worn just before killing his father. It was the same look he had turned on Brinna. And now here was Nola, trapped in the same house with Kirwyn, wearing Brinna's form—*being* Brinna, as far as anyone knew—and with a leg she couldn't walk on.

Don't worry yourself unnecessarily, Nola told herself. Even if Kirwyn wanted Brinna dead, even if he was actively plotting her murder, he wouldn't pick tonight, not the night after he'd killed his father.

But maybe that was the best time of all, Nola thought. People would think the intruder had come back. Maybe that was exactly the best time to commit a second murder.

"Lord Galvin," she called, stopping him at the door. "What about the killer?"

She could see him try to work out what she meant, since he had just clearly indicated to her that he suspected Kirwyn was the killer. She continued, "What if the killer comes back? Surely this household isn't safe. Will you and Sergeant Halig remain here tonight?" Galvin and Halig guarding the door had to be better than being trapped with Kirwyn, with only the too-trustful Alan to protect her.

Kirwyn snorted. "Timid Brinna. Surely that isn't necessary. The intruder has had the whole day to put Haymarket behind him while Lord Pendaran's men have squandered away the hours on pointless questions and frivolous searches."

If he hoped to shame Galvin into leaving, it was a mistake.

"Yes," Galvin told Nola. "We will be staying the night."

"This is a house in mourning," Kirwyn objected. "*With* a useless maid who has a crippled ankle. We do not have the wherewithal to put you up in a suitable manner."

"Then it is fortunate my needs are simple."

The crowd at the door parted for him, so that only Nola was in the room to see the look Kirwyn gave her as he muttered after Galvin, "Such as a useless maid with a crippled ankle?"

✿ CHAPTER THIRTEEN

THE LAST OF the people who had crowded around the doorway wished Nola well and closed the door behind them on their way to food and drink and reminiscing about Innis. Nola hastily put aside the hair she had plucked from Galvin's head. Her shoe would be a good hiding place, at least for now. Then she searched the blanket until she found one of Brinna's hairs, which she tossed into the cup of water she'd already bespelled.

Apparently all cried out, Brinna was asleep in the barn in which Nola had previously seen her. Nola even knew which barn it was, for it was so dilapidated that through the great chinks in the wall Nola could see the millpond. It was the barn in which she and her mother had considered staying—since it looked abandoned and probably had no one to order them out—when they had first come to Haymarket, before they stopped at the silversmith's house.

Brinna—asleep and alone. *You were lucky,* Nola told herself. *If she had been awake when the glamour wavered...*

Wavered?

WAVERED?

Nola had *abandoned* it for long enough that if Brinna had been aware of what was happening, she could have made her way to the house, could have been in among the funeral party before Nola had enough presence of mind to re-form the spell.

That didn't bear thinking about.

Besides, she had no time to spare on events she had already survived; she had to plan what to do next. She had arranged things so that she was—she hoped—safe from Kirwyn tonight. But those same arrangements had almost certainly assured that she would not be able to sneak out of the house once everyone was abed. Galvin and Halig would be keeping watch, to make sure no intruder came in, to make sure Kirwyn didn't leave his room to go to Brinna's. Certainly they were just as capable of noticing *her* going out.

In all likelihood, then, she was here for the duration of the night.

Once morning came she would have to convince them that she was fit enough to do the marketing. Alone. That was two obstacles to overcome: the convincing and the being able to walk at least as far as the outside door when moments ago she couldn't take one step unaided.

The room grew dimmer as late afternoon faded into evening, and finally the people who had attended Innis's funeral began to go home, and still, no better plan had suggested itself to Nola than to wait.

The cooper's daughters cleaned up after the guests. Either that or a hostile army set siege to the kitchen; it was hard to be sure about those rattlings and clatterings coming from down the hall.

When Alan came in bearing yet another tray of food, Nola asked about who had come and what she had missed, reasoning that without something to occupy her—besides, of course, keeping intact the spells that made her look like Brinna and Brinna look like her mother—she wouldn't be able to keep her eyes open much longer. Never mind that she didn't know any of the people that Alan might mention.

But Alan, stifling a yawn, claimed exhaustion and stayed only long enough to close the shutters against the night's dark and chill, using a piece of string, and never complaining that he would have to fix the broken latch.

Kirwyn came next.

Surely he wouldn't do anything, she tried to reassure herself. But she was becoming more and more convinced that Brinna had not made a simple mistake when she had claimed that the two of them were in the kitchen together during the time Innis was being attacked. And now, she guessed, he was here to persuade her not to change that story. By threat? By an appeal to love?

The first idea was distressing, the second disgusting.

Before Kirwyn had a chance to say anything, though, Galvin came up behind him and leaned over his shoulder. "Good night, Brinna," Galvin said. "Rest easy. I'll be in the kitchen, and Sergeant Halig will be in the shop, both of us alert for the faintest sound of trouble." Which was surely meant as much in warning as reassurance. He patted Kirwyn on the back and added, "Say good night, Kirwyn, and let her sleep."

"Good night, Brinna," Kirwyn said with a forced smile. "Perhaps by tomorrow you will be feeling well enough that I will not have to hire extra help to do your work for you."

She managed what was no doubt a sickly smile. She absolutely *must* not let herself get trapped alone in the house with Kirwyn.

Kirwyn slammed the door so hard that it shook.

She knew the night was going to last an eternity.

✿

LONG AFTER any reasonable person would have been asleep, Nola heard footsteps in the hall, coming from the direction of the other wing of the house—from the shop. The person was taking care not to make any extra noise, but what she heard were boots, not bare feet.

Surely Kirwyn would take more care than that.

The footsteps passed her door without pausing and entered the kitchen. She heard Halig's quiet voice ask, "Did you want to talk?"

Galvin must have whispered his answer, or not spoken aloud at all but simply gestured, for in a moment Nola heard the kitchen door open, then shut. Galvin apparently didn't want to take the chance that anybody else in the house was awake and listening.

Such precautions might protect him from the average eavesdropper, but...

Nola reached for the strand of his hair that she had tucked into her shoe.

She found herself hesitating. She had hoped—she had to admit to herself—to keep his hair, to be able to look in on Galvin one more time, later, when this was all behind her, when she could watch in safety for a good long time. She knew this was silliness. Besides, she *needed* to look now.

When the shadowshapes formed in the bespelled water, she saw that Galvin and Halig had stopped at the bench under the walnut tree in the courtyard. Galvin was sitting; Halig leaned against the tree. "I don't know what to make of her," Galvin said wearily.

"Could she have been trying to escape?" Halig asked. "Get to wherever they hid the money?"

So Galvin had told him about her misadventure with the window this afternoon, and more important, they suspected her—or rather, her-as-Brinna.

Nola clenched her hands in frustration that she had caused precisely what she had tried to prevent.

But Galvin shook his head at what Halig had said. "Hard to believe, given that she can barely make her way across a room. How far could she possibly have gotten?"

Their voices were quiet, and she had to strain to catch the words through the bespelled water. "It might be an act," Halig pointed out. In response to the look Galvin gave him at that, he added, "Well, part of it, at least. She could be exaggerating how badly she's hurt specifically so we don't watch her as closely as we should."

"She was on the floor," Galvin said. "I wouldn't have heard her leaving if she hadn't fallen."

Halig shrugged. "Maybe she didn't have far to go to get the money. Maybe she didn't even have to leave the room. Could it be hidden near the window, behind the shutters or beneath the sill?"

Again Galvin shook his head. "Not from what I could tell." And Nola remembered how he had considerately opened the shutters for her, even before helping her back to her feet.

Halig gazed off into the night, not looking at Galvin. He said, "So you're thinking she's what she seems and hasn't anything to do with the killing?"

Yes, Nola frantically thought. *Yes, yes, yes!*

Galvin sighed, which sounded much more like a *no,* even to Nola's energetic hoping.

Finally Halig faced him again. "That leaves Alan."

"I would very much prefer it to be Alan than Brinna," Galvin agreed.

Halig snorted and countered with, "I would very much prefer to be a rich baron, lord of a castle in the south."

Galvin rested his face in his hands.

You outrank him, Nola thought. *You can TELL him what to say.* But she knew this would not be settled by rank.

Halig said, "Kirwyn couldn't have done it alone, not the way they described it. One, if not both, of them is involved."

"I know," Galvin sighed.

Well, at least they were including Kirwyn in their suspicions.

"Alan…" Halig shook his head. "If I needed a partner, someone to lie for me, to help me, I would hate to be dependent on Alan's quick wits for something like that. It's much more likely to be her."

"She seemed to be *trying* to point us at Kirwyn."

I was! Nola thought at them.

Halig asked, "Are you thinking it was Brinna and Alan, and not Kirwyn at all?"

Nola would have liked to kick him.

Galvin shook his head impatiently. "Kirwyn is the one who stands to gain. We certainly have enough independent witnesses who say that father and son didn't get along well, even before this wedding was announced. It's just that Brinna…"

When his sentence drifted off into yet another sigh, Halig finished it for him: "Is so damned attractive."

"I was going to say brave," Galvin said, "brave even though she's obviously afraid—of us, of Kirwyn. How can such a beautiful young woman be so fearful of everything? I find myself wanting to reassure her. Don't," he added quickly, "even tell me. I know how simpleminded that sounds."

Halig raised his hands to indicate surrender.

Galvin continued, "She's funny. And spirited. And says such unexpected things. And she's kind; think of the way she responded to that woman, Crazy Mary."

"Mary," Halig repeated, as though that was the only significant thing Galvin had said. "Does she have anything to do with the murder?"

"I don't see how," Galvin answered.

Nola fervently hoped that meant they wouldn't be going after her mother, even though Nola had practically pointed a finger at her.

"The other choice," Halig said, once more gazing toward the street, though no one was walking by, "is to leave it. Report the silversmith was killed by an intruder, long gone by the time we arrived."

"Kirwyn is a murderer," Galvin said, aghast.

"But one who has what he wants. He's not apt to kill again."

It was a possibility. Not justice in any sense, but it was one possibility of safety for Nola among many chances of disaster.

Though Galvin didn't answer, Nola could see by his face that he wasn't going to agree to this.

Halig finally looked at him, returning his long, hard gaze. He said, "You'll never get Kirwyn without naming an accomplice."

"That's your counsel, is it?" Galvin asked coldly. "Put the blame on some passing brigand?"

"No," Halig told him. "But I would not contradict you if that's what you chose."

Galvin lowered his forehead to his clasped hands. Softly, miserably, he said, "I don't want to do that."

"What do you want?"

"To learn that Brinna is not a murderer."

"Most likely she's not," Halig agreed. "Most likely she only helped hide the money."

"But the money was probably hidden *before* the crime. There was no time afterward. So she knew what Kirwyn was planning and gave Innis no warning."

"There is that," Halig agreed.

Galvin sighed yet again. "And," he said, "I would like to finish this business without looking like a complete fool to Pendaran."

Halig grunted. "There, I can't help you at all."

Galvin stood. "I'll talk to her in the morning. Perhaps it would be best for you to be present, also."

Halig gave a curt nod.

As Galvin resettled in the kitchen and Halig made his way back to the silversmith's shop, Nola thought that she must come up with a better plan than trying to convince them that despite all the food brought in today, she urgently needed to go to the market first thing tomorrow morning.

He called me kind, Nola thought, which she'd never before thought of herself as. *And brave and funny.*

None of which was as good as being beautiful, but she wasn't used to *any* compliments.

Don't get distracted, Nola warned herself, realizing she was thinking more about Galvin than about getting out.

At best Galvin would eventually have to leave the premises, which would enable her to sneak away, and then she would never see him again.

At worst he would discover her true nature, and he would arrest her, and she would be banished or executed for witchcraft.

She hated stories with bad endings.

But she hesitated a long time before dragging Galvin's hair out of the water and ending the spell.

✪ CHAPTER FOURTEEN

T HE NIGHT LASTED longer than any night had a right to, but not long enough for Nola to come up with a plan she had any right to believe would work. Eventually—after she had been reduced to staying awake by amusing herself trying to balance a spoon on her nose—she could hear the stirrings of the household.

Once more she straightened her clothing and fetched her shoes from beside the bed. Did the right one go on easier than it had yesterday afternoon? *Yes,* Nola told herself, *definitely.*

Well, maybe.

She tried standing and decided that was easier, too. Or perhaps the ankle didn't hurt as much because she knew that this time she wouldn't have to try to walk quietly.

From the kitchen, she caught the crackle and smell of sausage frying and heard Alan—or Galvin if he was the kind to be inclined to help—setting the table. Halig came from guarding the door to the shop, and she could hear the sounds of Kirwyn stirring in his room.

Nola limped to the window and opened the shutters, untying the bit of string Alan had used to fasten them.

Over the courtyard fence, she could see the street; but no one was about this early. *Foolish plan,* she told herself. Everything depended on being lucky, and luck was certainly not something she had reason to rely on. But hoping for a passerby was the only plan she had been able to come up with all night long, and it wasn't likely something else would come to her now.

She hobbled back to the bed, intentionally pushing the night chest a bit so that it bumped the wall, and then started to straighten the blanket on her bed.

Galvin rapped against the door frame but didn't wait before he opened the door.

"Oh," Nola said, looking up from fluffing the mattress. "Good morning."

"What are you doing?" Galvin asked in a tone that was—she liked to think—testy because of concern rather than because of suspicion or lack of sleep.

"Straightening up the room," Nola said, rather than admitting the truth: *Making noise so in case you heard me getting up, you wouldn't think I was sneaking around.* Better to have him investigate now rather than later. She added with a smile, "One day of lying about in bed is enough." It was hard to sound so bright and cheery when her ankle throbbed and she hadn't slept in days.

Galvin glanced down at her feet, though of course her dress covered her ankle. "Are you sure you should be—"

"It's fine," Nola lied. "If I don't start moving, it's going to stiffen."

Kirwyn, coming down the hall from his room to the kitchen, paused only long enough to glance in over Galvin's shoulder. "It's about time," he said.

Once he had moved on, Nola blew a kiss after him, which made Galvin smile, and she remembered how he'd told Halig she was brave. The knowledge that she cared what Galvin thought made her blush, and she lowered her head to tug at a blanket that was already perfectly free of wrinkles.

"Don't try to do too much at once," Galvin advised. "Even Kirwyn can't expect you to take on all your usual chores so soon." Which showed he knew nothing about masters and servants. But Nola only smiled and nodded and worked very hard not to weep at the pain in her right leg.

As soon as he left, she sat down on the bed. But sitting, she couldn't see out the window into the street. So she struggled once more to her feet.

How long should she wait? she wondered, as she watched a young boy running on an early morning errand. But he was already gone before she had time to think. *Not long.* Someone running probably would have been a good choice, she thought. *If* the men took off in pursuit, they'd have a harder time catching up. But what were the chances of their looking up from their breakfast at just the right time to see such a person?

Obviously she needed someone walking from north to south—that is, someone following the street from the right side of Brinna's window to the left, which would bring them in view of the kitchen window only after passing Nola, because obviously she couldn't transform someone in plain view of the kitchen window when the whole plan hinged on the hope that *someone* would be looking out the window.

And she had to act fast, she reminded herself again as she spotted two young women walking together—in the wrong direction anyway—or the street would have too many people, and someone outside would see the transformation.

I can't be too particular, Nola told herself, guessing that Galvin, Halig, and Kirwyn must be finishing their breakfast, and that soon Alan would be knocking on her door, asking if she was coming out for hers or if he should bring it to her. Waiting for exactly the right person could doom the plan in any one of several ways, she thought.

And just as she thought it, exactly the right person walked into sight.

It was an old woman, walking from right to left—walking *slowly* because she had a cane. *Perfect.*

Fervently hoping no one else was watching, Nola said

the words of the transforming spell. She left the old woman her own clothes, but she gave her Brinna's face and hair.

The change caused no outcry, which was good, for this indicated no one on the street had noticed.

Look up, Nola wished at the men in the kitchen.

She waited, waited.

Had it been too long? Had the woman passed by the kitchen window unobserved? Should Nola change her back?

"Brinna?" It was Alan's voice. Good old Alan.

He *was* calling out the window, wasn't he—and not down the hall to her room?

"Brinna?" Alan's voice was louder this time. Definitely calling to someone who was moving away without heeding.

Nola heard the scrape of one of the benches as someone pushed away from the table.

"Brinna?" This time it was Kirwyn. Not tentative and amazed, as Alan's voice had sounded with the first calling of her name, nor even the second, louder attempt to get attention from a distance, but an angry bellow.

There was more noise from the kitchen. All four of the men put down cups, knives, plates—whatever they'd been holding—and got to their feet, scrambling to the window. Nola most intensely hoped it was all four men. The kitchen door opened, and she heard footsteps running, but it was impossible to tell how many pairs of feet.

She hesitated, ready to duck behind the bed in case any suspicious soul came to check the room.

But there were no footsteps coming down the hall. Either they had all taken off after the false Brinna or one or more of them were waiting in the kitchen to see what the others had to report, and if that was the case, her plan had failed of itself. She would not let it fail because she feared to act.

As she hobbled to Brinna's door, she let most of the transforming spell drop from the features of the old woman on the street before anyone had a chance to catch up to her. Nola left hair that was yellow rather than pure white and Brinna's very nose, so that the men would think themselves only foolishly deluded rather than tricked. She was growing less and less confident in her plan as time went by and her actions became irrevocable.

She was out Brinna's door and halfway down the hall before she heard the first sounds of the men returning through the courtyard. Actually, what she heard was Kirwyn saying, "Alan, you are such a fool. I have no idea why I put up with you."

Instantly Nola let entirely go of the glamour she had put on the old woman, and at the same time she turned around, faced *toward* Brinna's room, and transformed herself to look like her mother. "Brinna!" she called in a querulous voice. "Brinna's impostor! Where are you?"

Behind her, she heard the men enter the kitchen—in their rush to leave, they had not closed the door behind them.

She held on to the wall and didn't try to walk, for she didn't want them to see her limping. "I am the true Brinna!" she shouted. "Come out here and face me!"

From behind her, Kirwyn moaned, "Oh, not again!"

"Mary?" Alan edged past Kirwyn and gently took Nola's arm. "Hello, Mary. Have you lost Nola?"

Nola pulled her arm away. "I'm not looking for Nola. I'm looking for whoever that is who's pretending to be me. Can you see today that I'm Brinna?" Nola tossed her head to show off her wispy gray hair.

"Get this madwoman out of my house," Kirwyn demanded.

Alan glanced for direction not at Kirwyn but at Galvin and Halig—for which Nola was sure Kirwyn would make him pay later. Galvin, however, was looking quizzical. *He's wondering why Brinna hasn't come out of her room at all this bother,* Nola surmised.

And sure enough, the next moment he squeezed past Kirwyn and past Nola and Alan. "Brinna?" he called. When he saw there was no one there, he turned and looked at Nola.

"Gone?" Nola asked. "Good. I knew she couldn't keep up the pretense forever." She began humming and swaying. And hoping that she was making the situation better—not just more complicated.

Kirwyn practically knocked her down in his rush to Brinna's door. "That wasn't her on the street," he insisted. Was he needing assurance? Daring anyone to contradict him?

"No," Galvin agreed, still looking at Nola, still trying to figure out the connection. If Nola had been able to think of anyone besides Brinna whose appearance on the street she could be sure would get Galvin, Halig, Kirwyn, and Alan out of the house, she certainly would have tried that rather than risk what at best must seem a very odd coincidence. But the only other person that they all would recognize was Innis, and neither Galvin nor Halig struck her as the sort to believe in ghosts. And would Kirwyn have rushed out of the house to chase after the father he had killed?

Still, she was left with Galvin standing before her—and no doubt Sergeant Halig standing behind her—trying to resolve Brinna on the street/Brinna not on the street/Brinna not in her room/and old woman claiming to be Brinna.

Of all people, Kirwyn came to the rescue. He stormed past Galvin directly into Brinna's room, as though to make sure Brinna wasn't on the floor on the far side of the bed. "Brinna, you good-for-nothing whore!" he shouted, as though that would convince anyone who was hiding to come out. Although the blanket was neat and flat and obviously not covering anything, he yanked it off the bed, then flung it on the floor in frustration.

At least this tantrum distracted Galvin's attention away from her, though Nola worried that Kirwyn was furious enough to go after her. The other three would protect her, she assured herself. If there was time.

Kirwyn shoved the chest away from the wall, though

there was hardly room for a mouse back there. Muttering a stream of curses, he even threw open the lid of the chest, upending the dinner tray that was sitting on top. Then he kicked the cup and bowl out of his way.

"It *is* difficult to find a good housemaid," Galvin said amiably, as though that could be the cause of Kirwyn's ire.

For a moment Nola thought Kirwyn might go for his throat, but he quickly came to his senses, which might have had something to do with Halig taking a step forward.

"Maybe," said Alan, the peacemaker, "she left to do the marketing while we were occupied outside."

Nobody pointed out that Brinna supposedly couldn't take more than a step or two without aid. Nor that *if* Brinna had had a miraculous recovery, she would have come outside right on their heels, which surely one of them would have noticed when they turned back from their wild-goose chase after the old woman.

Kirwyn only said to Alan, "Out. Out of my house. You are useless, you always have been, you always will be—find employment elsewhere." And he stamped his feet like an outraged three-year-old, down the hall toward the silversmith's shop.

He turned back at the doorway to his father's room and pointed at Nola. "And get that old witch out of here, too!"

As always the word *witch* was almost enough to make

Nola's mind shut down in panic. She was barely aware of Kirwyn slamming the door. A moment later they heard him slam the door between the bedroom and the shop, too. And then, faintly, the outside door.

Galvin looked at Halig with raised eyebrows but wasn't going to say anything in front of outsiders. And at least they weren't looking at her. To Alan, who appeared ready to crumble at Kirwyn's dismissing him, Galvin said, "Don't leave. We need you here until the matter of this murder is settled."

Nola didn't wait for Alan's relief to settle in. She flung herself onto the floor saying, "And I'm not leaving, cither."

Galvin sighed. Though his tone indicated he suspected talking to her was useless, he asked her, "Do you know anything about Innis's death?"

Nola tugged at her hair in horror. "Innis is dead?" she cried. And she rocked back and forth, moaning loudly to make a nuisance of herself. "Oh, poor man, poor man." She didn't want to say anything to give them the idea that she knew anything useful, so she asked, "Has anyone told Kirwyn yet? First my mother died when she was giving birth to me, and now Master Innis. They always say death comes in threes. Who'll be next? Ohhh." She shuddered and put her hands up to cover her head.

Galvin asked Alan, "Do you know where she lives?"

Alan had knelt down beside her. "No," he said.

Nola howled louder. She hoped she was giving them

all headaches. "Nola!" she called, deciding it was time to drop the pretense that she thought she was Brinna. "Where's my daughter, Nola?"

Wincing at the noise, Halig asked Alan, "I don't suppose there's any chance you know where her daughter lives, either?"

"Madam," Galvin said as Alan shook his head, "please stop making that noise."

"I'm always noisy indoors," Nola shouted.

"If you don't stop," Galvin said, "we'll put you outdoors."

Far from being a threat, this was exactly what she had been hoping for.

"Noisy!" Nola leaned forward to shout at him.

His patience snapped. With a glance at Halig, who quickly interpreted it, Galvin moved forward and took Nola under the arms. Halig grabbed her legs. Nola went ahead and screamed at the pain of Halig's hand around her ankle.

Halig let go and made a helpless gesture, which Nola guessed was in response to an I-didn't-say-to-hurt-her glare from Galvin.

Lest they become suspicious about a second woman with an injured leg, Nola yelled at Halig, "Don't you become familiar with *me*, young man! I know you men are after only one thing!" She started screaming again so that she would be ready for the pain when Halig took her legs again.

They picked her up, gently, and brought her outdoors. As soon as they were out in the courtyard, she stopped screaming. "That's better," she said, trying to look pleased with herself though her ankle still throbbed.

She let Galvin and Halig set her down on the bench under the walnut tree.

"Can you fetch her something to eat?" Galvin said to Alan. "She doesn't look like she eats near enough."

Alan nodded.

"And then try to find the daughter." He stooped down to put himself on a level with her. "And you," he said, "behave yourself, or Master Kirwyn will fetch the magistrate."

Nola covered her mouth with both hands, as she had seen her mother do, and nodded earnestly.

Galvin gave a smile of encouragement that nearly broke Nola's heart. She had hoped that they would throw the crazy old woman out, and had not anticipated that they would take care with her. Galvin had told Halig that *she* seemed kind—well, he had said Brinna, but he meant Nola-as-Brinna. He, also, had seemed kind, but she had dismissed that as his trying to impress the beautiful Brinna. Now she had to fight to keep from leaning forward, from grabbing a handful of hair from off his head so that she would be able to, sometime, see him again.

But she couldn't take even one. She couldn't risk him connecting that with the time he had helped Brinna up from the floor of her room, and she had caught her finger on a hair and pulled it loose.

"And you and I," he was telling Halig, "will go in search of the elusive Brinna."

Halig nodded. He and Galvin were heading for the gate that led from the courtyard to the street, Alan was heading for the kitchen, and she would never see any of them again.

She closed her eyes and reminded herself that this was exactly what she had spent the whole last day trying to achieve.

✪ CHAPTER FIFTEEN

Although Nola wasn't in the least interested in food, she waited for Alan to fetch the promised meal so that he wouldn't see her leaving the garden. In fact, when he came out bearing a tray, she leaned against the tree, closed her eyes, and made a snoring noise so that he wouldn't feel obliged to chat with her.

She watched through slit eyes as he went out the gate after Galvin and Halig, who had gone out after Kirwyn, who was out looking for Brinna. Her ankle still hurt, but not enough to twist her stomach into a knot. She would be able to walk, she assured herself, at least as far as the wall.

There lay a pile of sticks and small branches and yard debris that had come down during the rain and wind of two nights ago. Nola found a long stick with which she could make do until she found a better one to use as a cane. And with that, she transformed herself yet again, this time giving herself the appearance of an old woman without choosing the face of any particular person of Haymarket.

She fought her inclination to simply head away from the chaos she herself had caused. She didn't know—not for sure—what Brinna's involvement was. Galvin had certainly proposed other wrong conjectures; she couldn't even tell which ones he actually believed plausible and which he set forth just to see what reaction they would get. Maybe there was another explanation to Brinna's claim to being in the kitchen with Kirwyn. Besides, Nola told herself, even if there wasn't—even if Brinna had conspired with Kirwyn to kill Innis—Nola *still* had used her badly, *still* owed her for kindness, *still* owed her explanations…still owed her a warning about Kirwyn.

With the walking stick helping to support her weight, Nola made her slow way to the river, to the barn that stood near the millpond. *This one chance,* Nola said. *If she's not there, so be it. I won't spend any time looking for her.*

She realized she was hoping Brinna wouldn't be there, for she couldn't get out of her head the picture of Innis lying on the floor.

The barn door creaked alarmingly.

There was a scurrying sound: slight, but too big for mice. Nola stood in the sagging doorway to let her eyes adjust. Despite the gaps in the walls through which morning sunlight streamed, there were areas of shadow. From one of these areas came Nola's mother's voice: "The walls are crumbling and the roof leaks, granny. But the mice are too timid to be much of a nuisance, and I'm willing to share what breakfast I have for news of the town."

Brinna.

Still being kind to strangers.

Nola let drop the transforming spells that made her look like an old woman and Brinna like her mother.

Brinna scrambled backward into a corner, which actually put her in more light than she had been in before. "You!" she gasped, seeing Nola's face emerge from the old woman's. But she heard the difference in her own voice and lifted her hands to see that they were once more, finally, her own.

"I'm sorry," Nola said. That wasn't nearly enough. "I'm very, very, very sorry." It would never be enough— not for all the fear she had caused. She herself had been afraid, but at least she had known what was going on, what her choices were, even if they weren't much. She was weak from lack of sleep and sore from her fall down the stairs, but at least her body had been under her own control.

"*Is* it truly you, Nola?" Brinna asked. And that, too, was Nola's doing: Brinna could never again be sure whether who she thought she was looking at was, in fact, who she actually *was* looking at.

"Yes," Nola said miserably. "Please let me explain—"

Brinna reached into the basket she had taken marketing with her, fetched out a crust of bread, and flung it at Nola, though it fell short. "Why did you do this to me?"

"I didn't mean you any harm," Nola assured her. "And I promise you, you'll suffer no lasting ill effects from it, and I won't do it again, and I'm sorry, but I was afraid, and I wasn't thinking properly, and it was the only way I could think of to keep us both out of danger." That *was* part of it. Nola took a step forward, and Brinna slid even further back into the corner, clutching the basket to her. For a moment Nola thought Brinna was about to fling more foodstuffs at her, but then she saw how tightly, how possessively, Brinna held the basket to herself.

How protectively.

Nola sighed.

Despite everything, she realized, she had still been hoping that Brinna hadn't been involved, that Brinna would explain all and somehow prove her innocence. Nola could hear the weariness in her own voice as she said, "That basket holds the money stolen from Innis, doesn't it? You and Kirwyn plotted together to kill him."

Brinna glanced down at the basket to make sure it was still covered, then her fear and anger bubbled over into derision. "Oh, and now you're going to chastise me for being a thief? You, a witch, taking advantage of people and disrupting their lives, stealing their very bodies? I think we've both made our choices, Nola, so don't you look down at me."

"I'm not," Nola said, though she felt the criticism wasn't entirely fair: Brinna had chosen to become a thief;

Nola had never been offered a choice about being a witch.

But she had chosen to *use* her witchcraft, so maybe that was the same.

"I didn't kill Innis," Brinna objected.

Nola didn't say, "I know," for then she would have to explain that her witchcraft went beyond changing appearances.

Brinna said, "I didn't even steal this." She indicated the basket. "Kirwyn stole it," she said. "He knew where Innis kept the strongbox, under one section of the floor, and then he found where Innis had the key hidden. He emptied out the box and gave the things to me to hide. So this was *given* to me. I didn't *steal* it."

Their plan made sense: Brinna could take the money away from the house and hide it somewhere while Innis was busy working, never suspecting his son would kill him that evening, and meanwhile all the neighbors, all the customers could swear that Kirwyn had never left the shop all that day long.

But it was still stealing, whatever Brinna said. And murder: Brinna had known of Kirwyn's plan in time to warn Innis if she had wanted to.

"What did Innis ever do to you?" Nola asked.

"Nothing," Brinna admitted. "But he was old, and he'd been wealthy all his life. And then he decided to get a young bride. And a common maid wouldn't do for him. I was good enough to help him pass the time, but when he wanted a *wife*, to produce another *heir*, he went and asked a wealthy wool merchant's daughter from Linchester. The two of them would have had more money than they knew what to do with. And would she have left me to continue working in her new husband's house, a potential rival? I think not. After running that household so smoothly for the past two years, I would have been knocking on doors, begging for a chance to be a scullery maid again."

Nola sighed. "I didn't come to hear this. I came to warn you about Kirwyn. I tried to act like you, to say the things I thought you would say. But I didn't realize you…" It was hard to say. "…had helped Kirwyn. Because he thought I was you, and because of the way I was acting, he's become suspicious of you. I truly believe he means you harm."

Brinna snorted. "Well, he would have gone to the…" She looked suspiciously at Nola. "Well, never mind, to the place where I hid this." Again the glance at the basket. "But I went back there myself—after you worked your *witchcraft* on me." That was probably meant as a reminder that Nola was in no position to tell anybody what she knew—which she had no intention of doing, anyway. "And I took it with me. Because *I* didn't know, either. For all I could tell, you and Kirwyn had come to an agreement without me." Nola must have made a face, for Brinna laughed. "Why did you ever return to Haymarket anyway?" she asked bitterly. "Why did you pretend to be me?"

"It makes no difference," Nola said. "And once I got here, my only intent was to get away." She noticed that Brinna didn't ask about Nola's mother, nor about why Nola needed a crutch. And why should she? Nola was not her concern. But Nola would have asked. Nola finished, "And this time, I won't be back. I just wanted you to know about Kirwyn. You might want to try telling him that you were only trying to distract Galvin so that he wouldn't become suspicious."

"Galvin? *Galvin,* is it? Oh, we've been flirting with Lord Pendaran's men, have we?"

Nola tried to ignore the question, though she felt her face go warm. "The important thing is that you don't trust Kirwyn. I believe he may have been planning you ill long before I came into the situation."

Brinna got to her feet, which probably would have been easier to do if she hadn't been clutching the basket to her chest with such obvious distrust, as though Nola might yet make a grab for it. The thing must have been heavy: Once she settled it on her arm, Nola saw how low she held her elbow. "No doubt," Brinna said. "I don't intend to give him the chance."

She had already passed Nola and was almost to the door before Nola called after her, "What do you mean?"

Brinna raised her arm with the basket. "He has the house and the shop with everything in it. After all I've been through, he can't very well begrudge me this…" She tossed her head so that her golden hair caught in the sunlight, and she walked out of the barn.

"Good luck," Nola told her, but she was already gone.

She gave Mother and me a job when no one else would, Nola reminded herself.

Though now she wondered if the plan had been to let one of them get blamed for the murder.

She gave us food when we left. There could have been no possible advantage to Brinna in that.

Still, she had a long way to travel and she already felt weary. She leaned heavily on her walking stick as she made her way out of the barn.

Brinna was by the millpond, talking to a man who was coming from the mill with a sack of flour over his shoulder. She was pointing beyond the mill to where the river continued on its way south. Nola saw Brinna hand the man something, probably a coin, and the man, nodding, led her to where his small rowboat was tied.

He rearranged the sacks that were already in the boat, then helped Brinna in. The boat rocked and she sat down hastily. The man laughed and said something, probably to reassure her. People were always solicitous of the beautiful, Nola had come to see. The man pushed off from shore, the boat scraping noisily against the stones at the water's edge, riding low in the water because of the extra weight.

It would be nice, Nola thought, if she, too, had a ride to where she was going. But since she didn't, she'd better start walking.

She estimated that with her sore ankle, the journey would take her a day and a half.

And what could her mother have gotten up to in all this time?

Before Nola had a chance to turn onto the path, a voice sounding no farther than a handspan from her ear shouted, "Brinna!"

Nola shrank back from Kirwyn, though he didn't seem to recognize her—nor even to notice her.

"Brinna!" He had paused on the path itself, but now he cut through the grass, heading for the water's edge. Brinna and the man who was rowing both turned to face him. "Brinna, you faithless creature! You get back here!"

The man hesitated, but Brinna said something to him, and he kept rowing.

"Brinna!" Kirwyn bellowed. "I know you have my money!"

When they still didn't head back for shore, Kirwyn picked up a stone from the shore and flung it. In his fury, he threw it so hard it went way over the heads of the boaters. He picked up another stone, and that fell short, thudding against the side of the boat.

"Hey!" called the boat's owner. "Enough of that!"

Other people, seeing the commotion from the street, called out, too: some in reproach, some in encouragement.

Kirwyn threw another stone, which hit Brinna on the arm.

They were still close enough to shore that Nola could see the pain and surprise on her face as she rubbed her arm. And the fear.

"Enough of that, you!" the boat's owner shouted.

At the same time another voice called, "Kirwyn!"

And there was Galvin, running down the path toward them.

Nola, who had never expected she would see him again, ducked her head.

But of course he didn't recognize her. He couldn't have: He'd never seen her face before. He ran to intercept Kirwyn, who was picking up another stone.

Kirwyn's aim was thrown off when Galvin grabbed hold of his arm. "She killed my father," Kirwyn protested. "She stole his money."

He would have to do better than that, Nola thought, considering the previous story he had told.

"Leave off," Galvin warned. And, to the man in the boat he said, "You, come back."

Brinna leaned forward to tell the man something that made him hesitate.

Kirwyn picked up another stone.

Galvin caught hold of his wrist. "Put it down now, or I'll seriously consider cutting your hand off," he said, though he hadn't yet unsheathed his sword.

Kirwyn let the stone drop.

The man in the boat still hadn't made up his mind whether to come back to shore. "In the name of Lord Pendaran—," Galvin called to him, but his forward momentum brought him onto that part of the bank that was both inclined *and* covered by stones. One foot slid so that he had to catch his balance, and this brought him just beyond Kirwyn, and slightly lower.

And Kirwyn had quite obviously had enough of being bested by Brinna and Galvin. While Galvin was distracted by boat and footing, Kirwyn took advantage of being temporarily higher and jabbed his elbow, catching Galvin on the side of his head.

As Galvin staggered, Kirwyn hooked his leg around Galvin's and the next moment Galvin was on the ground with Kirwyn astride his back.

"Stop!" Nola cried. There were several onlookers close enough to help, but none of them stepped forward, though one of them did say—mildly, considering the circumstances—"Hey, now." Nola hobbled painfully toward the two struggling men, her makeshift cane sliding off the slippery stones, jarring her aching ankle.

Kirwyn snatched up another of the river stones and brought it down on Galvin's head. Once. Twice. Just as he had done when bringing the hammer down on Innis.

But Galvin was quicker than Innis had been, and he was fighting back: The blows were only glancing.

Still, Kirwyn was on top, and it was only a matter of time before he got in a good hit that would crack Galvin's skull open.

Nola raised her walking stick and brought it down hard across the small of Kirwyn's back.

With a yelped curse, he rolled off Galvin and glared

at Nola. Then he looked at the stone in his hand. Then he glared at Nola again.

Still nothing from the onlookers. In fact, a few of them backed away.

Kirwyn surged to his feet.

Nola remembered all the blood that had seemed to fill the water basin when she had watched Kirwyn smash in Innis's skull. That was what he was about to do to her—she was sure of it. He was going to kill her while Galvin was just now sitting up, obviously not quite able to get his eyes to focus yet, too groggy to intervene. *If* he even noticed her danger.

But Kirwyn didn't go after her. He looked at the stone he'd been striking Galvin with, then he looked once more at Brinna in the boat. The man she was with had started toward the shore in response to the authority in Galvin's voice, but had stopped rowing when Kirwyn had attacked Galvin. Now the man hurriedly resumed rowing—away once again.

Kirwyn flung the stone with all his might at Brinna. It hit her on the side of her head.

From the shore, it looked as though she tried to stand up, possibly in a confused attempt to get away. The man who had been rowing dropped his oars and lunged for her, to get her to sit back down.

Too late.

The boat tipped, and Brinna, the man, and all those sacks of flour went into the water. The man bobbed up to the surface. The way he floundered and scrambled to clutch on to the capsized boat gave testimony to the fact that he was not a swimmer. There was no sign of Brinna.

Galvin finally staggered to his feet.

"Go!" a voice yelled, and it was Sergeant Halig, who—a moment later—caught hold of Kirwyn and twisted his arms behind his back. "Go," he repeated to Galvin. "I can't swim."

"She deserved it," Kirwyn said.

Nola looked at him in horror, but he had lost all hope of getting away with what he had done and offered no more pretenses.

Galvin ran out into the water as Halig deftly tied Kirwyn's hands behind his back. Two of the onlookers at last were stirred to action, and they, too, headed for the water.

"She deserved it," Kirwyn repeated.

"Oh, shut up," Nola told him.

One of the two onlookers who'd jumped into the millpond caught hold of the shirt of the floundering boatman and dragged him to shore, while Galvin and the other man dived repeatedly beneath the surface. And still there was no sign of Brinna.

"Lots of water weeds," the rescuer said from between chattering teeth as someone put a blanket around his shoulders. "And the water's damn murky." The words were quickly passed through the ever-growing crowd.

"She deserved it," Kirwyn said again, this time only daring a mutter.

Halig smacked him on the back of the head.

Others joined the two men out in the water. It seemed forever, but, eventually, all together, they came swimming back, dragging something behind them.

Nola had hoped that somehow Brinna had gotten away, that she'd succeeded in swimming underwater— never mind that her waterlogged skirts would surely have dragged her down. Nola had refused to let her mind settle on that detail. She had pictured Brinna making it to the edge of the pond and hiding in the reeds, ready to make her escape.

They brought her up on shore right near where Nola had sat when her leg had begun shaking from the strain of so much walking and standing. Even if Brinna hadn't been underwater for so long, Nola would have known she was dead by the way her beautiful blue eyes stared up unblinking at the sun. Galvin sat down cross-legged beside her, his own eyes closed, his head bowed.

One of the others extended his arm, holding out Brinna's marketing basket, from which water still streamed. He indicated by lowering and raising it several times that it was heavy. "She was still holding on to this," he said. "It weighted her down to the bottom."

"That's mine," Kirwyn said.

Someone asked, "Was she dead already from the blow to her head before she went into the water, or wouldn't she let go, and then she drowned?"

Different people had different opinions and were open about sharing them.

"That's mine," Kirwyn repeated. "She stole it from me."

Galvin jumped to his feet, snatched the basket out of the man's hand, and flung it at Kirwyn, scattering coins all about the grass. Then, without a word, he stalked away, heading back toward the center of town.

Abashed, the people on the grass silently gathered up the fallen money and replaced it in the basket, then handed the basket to Halig. "Much pleasure may it give you in your remaining time," Halig told Kirwyn, and gave him a shove in the direction Galvin had gone.

Nola stood up, requiring much help both from her walking stick and from the woman next to her. As the townsfolk resumed their speculations, Nola started walking, too, but in the opposite direction.

✿ CHAPTER SIXTEEN

It ended up taking Nola five days to get back to Saint Erim Turi.

By midafternoon of that first day, she was able to take only nine steps at a time—counting them off, always starting and ending with her uninjured left foot: Only four more, only three—before she'd allow herself to rest, leaning on her good left leg and her stick, breathing raggedly, her ankle swollen to twice its size, burning and throbbing. She finally understood those stories of an animal biting off its own injured foot. And she'd gotten only as far as the outlying farms of Haymarket.

She was considering whether it would be better to abandon the stick and crawl on the road when a farmer working the adjoining field called out to her. "You look like you need some help."

By chance the farmer and his family needed help, too. The man's wife had just had a baby, to go along with what seemed to be about seventeen other small children, who ran in and out of the house, chasing one another, climbing on things, poking each other, until *somebody* ended up squealing or crying—although once all of them were put to bed, it turned out there were only five of them. Still exhausted from her labor, the farmer's wife needed someone to keep the children from inflicting permanent damage on themselves, one another, or the house.

Nola planned to start again the next morning, after a blessed night's rest. But, "If you could help around the house—," the farmer's wife said, then, gazing down at Nola's foot, she assured her, "mostly sitting-down work—my husband and I could take you almost all the way to Saint Erim Turi in four days' time, when we take the baby to show my parents."

Four days, Nola thought. Leave her mother untended for four more days? But what could she do? Unless she was lucky enough to get someone else to offer her a ride, at the rate she was going these people would pass her by on the road four days from now. And she'd probably be permanently crippled by then. She could only hope that her mother would stay safe. She hoped that Galvin was safe also. She would picture the look on his face by the millpond, when he knew he had lost Brinna forever, and she knew her face tended to the same expression for losing *him.*

So she helped with the cooking and the mending of clothes and the settling of squabbles among the children, and four days later—with grateful hugs and tears of good-bye—the farmer and his family dropped Nola off on the outskirts of Saint Erim Turi, with a full stomach, an ankle that had finally begun to heal, and a proper walking stick that the husband had fashioned for her.

But Nola also had a growing dread, now that the end was in sight, of what she'd find in Saint Erim Turi in general, and at the Witch's Stew tavern in particular.

She paused before the first cluster of houses, just a heartbeat's hesitation before stepping under the huge oak tree that sprawled its branches like a canopy over the road. *It must have rained here,* she thought, noticing how wet the ground beneath the tree was, and in that pausing she missed being hit directly on the head by something falling from overhead. Instead, it fell at her feet and burst open: a pig's bladder filled with water.

"You miserable wretches!" she yelled at the four laughing, squealing children who hid in the branches above her. Two of them leaped down and took off into the surrounding bushes. The other two were old enough to know better.

"Mother!" Nola cried. "What are you doing up there?"

Still laughing, her mother said, "It seemed like a good idea at the time. But I do believe Modig is stuck."

How the old man and his cane had gotten up a tree, Nola didn't even ask. Nor did he volunteer the information, though he did tell about the time he and some of the other young men of the king's army had treed a bear.

Eventually they got him down. The two playmates who had previously abandoned them came back to offer encouragement and suggestions, as did several other of the townschildren. Modig, it turned out, had become very popular with the children, with all the stories he had to offer of times gone by and traveling to different lands. He challenged Nola to a cane-dueling contest, and Nola, who was frantic to talk to her mother alone, was relieved when her mother told him, "Women's talk," and took Nola's arm and led her away.

"Is everything all right?" Nola demanded as they walked toward the tavern.

"With me?" her mother asked, as though the question was an odd one. "Fine. How about you?"

Nola ignored the matter of her twisted ankle and her broken heart. "I managed to empty the bucket before anyone saw the spell," she said.

"Yes," her mother said.

"And the authorities know it was Kirwyn who killed his father."

"Yes," her mother said.

"The sad part is that I never realized Brinna was involved, that she'd helped Kirwyn. She took some of Innis's money away to make everyone think an intruder had killed Innis for his wealth, when it was really Kirwyn, to keep him from remarrying." Nola took a deep breath. "And then Kirwyn killed Brinna."

Her mother gave her hand a comforting pat. "Yes," she said.

Peeved that her mother didn't seem more surprised— or interested—Nola asked, "Is there anything you'd like to know about where I've been or what I've been doing?" She thumped her walking stick—though as soon as she did, she remembered it was something Modig had a tendency to do. But she wanted to make sure her mother noticed she'd been hurt, though she couldn't see how her mother had missed it, especially since Modig had wanted a cane duel.

Her mother didn't ask about Nola's ankle. She asked, "So why did you let that good-looking young man go?"

Nola stopped walking. "*What* good-looking young man?" she demanded, knowing that her mother couldn't mean what it sounded as though she meant.

But she did. "Pendaran's man: Galvin. That Sergeant Halig wouldn't have been bad, either—not in a pinch—but Galvin was obviously smitten with you."

Nola had trouble getting her mouth to work. "What— How—" She had to take a steadying breath. "How do you know about this?"

The question obviously amazed her mother. "From watching you."

"*What?*"

"Shhh." Her mother glanced around to make sure Nola wasn't attracting people's attention. She tugged on her arm to get her walking again. "You have to be more careful, dear," she said.

"What do you mean, *watching* me?" Nola demanded.

"Well, what do you think?" her mother countered. "You left your hairbrush."

Nola yanked her arm out of her mother's grip and

clapped her hands over her hair. "You've been *spying* on me? You've been watching me while I haven't known it?"

As if that wasn't bad enough, her mother acted as though Nola was dull-witted. "Well, you should have guessed."

Nola supposed she should have, given that her mother was the one who had taught her to bespell water. "Don't *ever* do that again," Nola said.

"All right." Her mother agreed so amiably that Nola knew she would always do exactly what she felt like doing.

But there was no more time for talking, for they had reached the tavern, the Witch's Stew, and Nola knew they couldn't have this conversation in public. She still didn't know what her mother had been up to in her absence—besides dropping pig bladders from tree branches to soak unsuspecting passersby—but, all in all, it would undoubtedly be best to leave Saint Erim Turi as quickly as possible. "Gather your things," Nola told her, walking around the barrel-filled wagon that was parked out front. "We're leaving."

"But I like this place," her mother protested as Nola opened the door.

"Mother...," Nola said. But then she stopped, for sitting at one of the tables were Galvin and Halig.

Still, for the moment they hadn't seen her. Better yet, they hadn't seen her mother, whom they would recognize—or *think* they recognized.

Edris the tavern keeper was just coming up from the

cellar, where the barrels of beer and wine were stored, and this would have been fine but for one thing: Accompanying her were the blackberry farmer and his wife, from Low Beck.

Nola took a quick step backward, dragging her mother with her.

Her mother gave a little yelp of surprise. "Galvin and Halig!" She turned to Nola as the two men looked up. "So you *did* tell them where to find you." She told the men, "I was just saying to Nola she could do worse than either one of you."

The men exchanged a startled look. And—oh, yes—Nola could tell they definitely recognized her mother.

Meanwhile, Edris was just recognizing her, was just smiling and saying, "Welcome back, Nol—"

But by then the blackberry farmer's wife had looked to see what was happening. "You!" she said. Then she saw Nola's mother. "And you!"

Her mother threw her hands up to cover her face. "Surely you have us mistaken for someone else," she said, starting to back up. "Come, Nola."

But by then it was too late. The farmer's wife turned to Galvin and Halig. "It's them! The ones you were sent to arrest."

❈ CHAPTER SEVENTEEN

Aᴀғᴛᴇʀ ᴀʟʟ sʜᴇ'ᴅ been through? She and her mother were going to get arrested for something that wasn't their fault?

Halig spoke. "We were sent to *question*," he corrected the woman.

Nola tried to judge Galvin's expression, which seemed less friendly than the sergeant's.

He's probably weighing the likelihood of running into the same madwoman in two subsequent and supposedly unrelated matters, Nola thought. He looked, she was relieved to see, as though he had taken no lasting hurt from Kirwyn's attack.

Of course, he didn't recognize *her* without Brinna's form. He could hardly stand to look at her in her true face. His gaze slid right off her and back to the complaining woman, who was now explaining to Edris, "We hired those two women to pick berries..." Her husband for some reason was shaking his head, but the woman only got louder. "But they broke a fine jug of ours and walked off with a bushel basket of berries."

A basket of berries?

"It *is* them," the woman insisted.

"It's not," the man mumbled.

"I recognize them." She pointed at Nola and her mother. "Thieves," she said. "I remember you because you waited in the yard while I prepared a fine lunch for your midday meal. I felt sorry for you, so we took you on even though you *looked* dishonest. But you hardly worked at all, so that halfway through the morning when my husband went to check if all was well with you, you'd broken the water jug he left you and stolen off with the lunch *and* a whole basketful of blackberries."

The false accusations stung. "That's not true," Nola said.

"It's not them," the husband murmured. What was this uncharacteristic meekness? Then Nola realized: He didn't want trouble; he didn't want anyone looking too closely at the story he had told his wife.

And to think how much time I spent worrying about him! Nola thought. *Big-talking coward who knows he can fool his wife but doesn't want to take on the authorities or be face-to-face with the accused.*

"I reported it to the town magistrate," the woman said in a self-satisfied tone, as though that was proof of guilt. "And these men have been sent to arrest you, you lazy, good-for-nothing thieves."

Surely Galvin wouldn't believe this, Nola assured herself.

But, then, why shouldn't he?

Still, so far neither Galvin nor Halig had reacted. They were just watching and listening.

"We didn't break that jug," Nola told them. "And we took no basket of berries." *They don't know it's you,* she told herself. They wouldn't know to be on the lookout for lies. All she'd ever done was lie to them, and now the truth sounded false to her ears. To the woman, she said, "We didn't even eat your stingy little lunch, because we had to run away to be rid of your groping husband."

The woman gave a cry of disbelief that anyone could say such a thing. "We've been bringing blackberries here for the blackberry wine for eleven years," she said. "And nobody yet has called us liars. Edris, tell how you know us."

"I...," Edris said, then tactfully finished, "wouldn't call any of you liars."

Finally Galvin was getting to his feet, and the woman from Low Beck, obviously unsatisfied with Edris's answer, pointed at Nola and her mother and said, "These women took advantage of our hospitality."

Galvin barely glanced at Nola, which surely was a bad sign. "You hired these two women to work for you picking berries?" he asked the woman.

"Yes, and they broke—"

"And you paid them before they did the work?"

"Yes. Well, I made them lunch."

Galvin glanced back at Nola with his customary unreadable expression. He asked the woman, "So they were to work all day picking berries in exchange for lunch."

"Well, the morning was half gone before they even showed up at my doorstep, begging."

"But you just said your husband went to check on them halfway through the morning."

For the first time, Nola thought maybe Galvin wasn't as disinterested as he acted. She glanced at Halig, who was still sitting at their table, looking as though he was enjoying this.

The woman flapped her hand in a nervous, dismissive gesture. "I didn't mean *exactly* midmorning."

"I see," Galvin said. He looked at the man. "Do you agree with all your wife has said—barring, of course, the exactness of midmorning?"

The farmer shuffled his feet. "They said they'd work, and they didn't." A definite shift from "It's not them."

Once more Galvin turned his attention to Nola. "But you say the man tried to force his attention on you. And that you don't know anything about the broken jug."

"I said we didn't break the jug," Nola corrected him. "He himself dropped the jug when I kicked him to get away from him."

Galvin looked at her foot, at the walking stick she held. "That would be before you injured yourself?" he observed, just as the woman was sputtering, "That's absurd."

Nola nodded to indicate Galvin was right: She had hurt her ankle *after* kicking the farmer. And surely he must be thinking of Brinna now, remembering her injured leg, remembering…

Galvin held up a hand to command silence from the farmer's wife. "And what do you say?" he asked Nola's mother.

"None of us liked the way he was looking at our Nola," her mother said.

"Look at her!" the woman protested. "She's a skinny little nothing! My husband would have nothing to do with her."

Far from being upset that she had talked out of turn, Galvin asked pensively, "So, you're saying he might have forced his attention on her if she was…more attractive?"

Galvin's turning the woman's own words on herself was a relief to Nola, but the comment still stung.

"No!" the woman said. She jabbed her elbow at her husband. "Tell him."

But before the man could tell anything, Nola took a chance, for she had nothing to lose. She said, "The sister-in-law was attractive. You might ask her."

The man's jaw worked a bit before he could get out a single, strangled "I…," and then gave up.

His wife looked at him in horror.

Galvin studied the man appraisingly, then asked Nola, "Where did you kick him?"

"Left knee," Nola said.

Again he evaluated her injured leg, which, standing

face-to-face, would have been the one she was most likely to use to kick someone's left leg. But instead of pressing her, he asked the man, "Care to show us your left knee?"

"It was all a misunderstanding," the farmer said.

His wife's expression of horror seemed to be set.

Galvin kept pressing. "But you told the magistrate. It's against the law to lodge false complaints with the magistrate."

"I'm sorry," the man said. "It wasn't exactly a false complaint—"

"Ah, *exactly*, again," Galvin said.

"It was a *misunderstanding*," the man repeated lamely. "And it was my wife who reported it."

His wife gave him a good hard kick on the same knee Nola had kicked the previous week. *"That,"* she said, "you will pay for. A good, long time you will pay for it." She stamped out of the tavern.

"Speaking of paying…," Galvin said, and nothing more until the man drew a few coins from his pocket, which he placed in Nola's mother's hand.

Galvin made a show of looking, then said, as though surprised, "Hmm." He glanced at Halig, who shook his head dubiously. The farmer hastily added more.

"See you don't lodge another misunderstanding with the magistrate," Galvin warned him.

"No," the man assured him, obviously relieved that he was being let off easily. "Thank you. I won't." He fled after his wife, though his back must have scraped the wall in his attempt to stay clear of Nola.

Edris, beaming, told Nola and her mother, "Good for you! But I don't dare lose them as providers of blackberries for our wine. Let me just try to smooth things over."

Sergeant Halig drained the last of his drink. "I'll stand around and intimidate them a bit, shall I?" he asked Galvin. But as he passed Nola's mother, who was trying to balance the coins on her fingertips, he smiled, nodded, and asked, "Feeling better, Mary?"

"Than what?" she asked. And while he paused over that, she added, "And my name is Cleopatra."

Halig sighed. "Never mind." And he went outdoors, leaving Nola and her mother alone with Galvin.

Galvin was giving her mother a wary look, but he had a smile for Nola. "I recognize you," he said.

There was no way he could.

"From the town of Haymarket," he explained. "You rescued me." And when she continued to gaze at him blankly, he said, "From Kirwyn, Innis's son. On the bank of the millpond."

"Oh," Nola said. She held up her walking stick, though it had been her previous stick with which she had struck Kirwyn. Just the mention of Haymarket, the memory that had to bring of the dead Brinna, made Galvin look drawn and strained, she thought.

She couldn't stand this any longer, knowing that he had liked her only because she looked like Brinna, knowing that—even if he found her kind and brave and all those other nice things he had called her—he wouldn't have thought so if she hadn't temporarily been beautiful. "My mother and I were just leaving," she said.

"No, we weren't," her mother said. She dropped the coins down the front of her dress, even though several fell right back out again.

Galvin pretended not to notice. He said, "I have recommended to Lord Pendaran that since Innis the silversmith had no close kin beyond Kirwyn, the shop should be handed over to the assistant, Alan." He paused to consider, then added, "Just in case you know these people."

Nola's mother smacked Nola on the back of the head.

Galvin raised his eyebrows, waiting.

"Ahm...," Nola said. She realized that what her mother meant was, *Say something to him*. She would, if she could think of something. She said, "Thank you. For getting to the truth with..." She nodded her head vaguely outdoors.

Galvin shrugged. "I didn't think you looked like thieves."

Seeing her mother was about to say something, Nola clapped her hand over her mother's mouth.

Galvin looked from one of them to the other. By his expression, Nola judged that he considered at least several possible responses before finally answering, "Well, good-bye."

She would never see him again.

She had thought so twice before, but now she knew this was absolutely her last chance. She could go on living the way she had been, or she could try to hold on to Galvin.

But what if his comments to Halig in the garden weren't true? What if it wasn't *her* that he liked but Brinna's appearance?

Still, if she didn't trust him, she'd never know.

She said what she'd spent all her life hiding, what she'd been afraid a moment ago her mother would say. She said, "We're not thieves. We're witches."

Again Galvin gazed from one to the other. Steadily. He said, "Obviously."

Which left Nola with nothing to say. He *knew*?

Nola's mother said, "My husband likes the looks of you and thinks you can be trusted. Here. Listen." She put her head up close to his.

That, at least, flustered him. He cast an anxious glance at Nola.

Her mother continued. "And *I* think you have possibility, too. I've always told Nola, 'Never underestimate someone who's willing to hold your head while you're being sick.'"

Maybe, Nola thought, he wouldn't remember.

But she could hear the breath he took in, and his face, which she'd already thought pale, went white.

Nola's mother caught hold of one of the chairs and moved it behind Galvin, who sat down heavily. "My husband said you looked a bit unsteady," she said.

Galvin looked at her, at Nola, back at her, before he

started breathing again. "Perceptive fellow," he managed to whisper. He hardly had better control over his voice when he asked Nola, "Brinna?"

"No," she said. "Well…" She buried her face in her hands. "Sometimes."

So she told him.

Everything.

From picking blackberries in Low Beck, to accidentally looking in at Innis's murder, to returning to the house, to meeting him and Sergeant Halig, to bespelling Brinna, to falling down the stairs, to finally getting out of the house, to watching helplessly while he and the townsfolk tried to find Brinna's body in the millpond.

She didn't, of course, tell him that her heart had hurt worse than her ankle at the thought that she would never see him again.

"So it was you," he said softly, "all the while…"

"Not all the while," she corrected him. "You did meet the true Brinna first."

"But all the while…" He stopped himself.

Still she felt sure she knew what he'd been going to say.

And she was just as sure she knew why he wouldn't let himself say it.

She was an admitted witch. He would have to turn her in. She remembered the conversation she had overheard in the garden between Galvin and Halig, when Halig had suggested that Galvin could ignore his suspicions about Brinna. Galvin had refused, because his sense of justice was stronger than whatever he felt for Brinna. Nola braced herself for his declaring that she and her mother were both under arrest.

But he didn't say that. Instead, he said, "I won't tell."

She said, "But…" She heard her mother give a groan of exasperation, but Nola couldn't leave it at that. "You refused to ignore that Brinna helped Kirwyn kill his father."

"It's not the same," he said.

She could see it wasn't. He hadn't been surprised to hear they were witches. He'd had his suspicions, at least from today, if not earlier, and he wasn't going to turn them in.

"I don't see," he told her, "that you cause harm to any."

"No," she agreed breathlessly. What more could she ask for? He was giving her her life and her mother's. That should be more than enough to satisfy a witch who had both a plain face and no reason to believe in luck.

And yet she remembered how he'd looked at her while she'd worn Brinna's face, and she started to say, "I could look like her again." But she knew that was wrong. For any one of several reasons. She bit back the offer before she got her mouth fully around the initial "I—," and ended with a sound like a strangled gasp.

Galvin stood, hurriedly, and took her arm as though to steady her. "Are you all right?" he asked.

"A bit light-headed," she said, which was only the smallest part of it. He was just being kind, she reminded herself.

Galvin gave that smile that made her knees weak. "If you're going to be sick," he told her, "I'll hold your head." Emphatically, he finished, "But I will not sing."

Even to her, it sounded like more than just being kind.

She wondered if he would have noticed her without Brinna's face. But the fact was, he *had* noticed her.

So why didn't he say so?

He wasn't sure, she suddenly realized. All this while—despite herself—she'd been growing to love him. But he couldn't know that. He didn't dare assume she felt anything for him. So she told him. She said, "I was afraid I'd never see you again."

But he didn't put his arms around her and tell her that love would conquer all. He pulled away from her and narrowed his eyes suspiciously, putting together things she had said. "Were you watching me? Did you ever do this bespelling of water to see *me*?"

It was not a part of the story that had seemed to need to be told. But she wouldn't lie to him. She had told enough lies for a lifetime. "Yes," she admitted.

"You *spied* on me?" She recognized the exact tone of outrage she had used while accusing her mother of the very same thing.

"Yes," she said. "Just once. While you were talking in the garden, with Sergeant Halig."

The fact that he had been doing nothing wrong nor potentially embarrassing apparently wasn't enough. "Don't *ever* do that again," he told her. "I would hate to have to shave my head just to ensure privacy."

"I'll never do it again," she promised.

Then, finally, he pulled her in closer for an embrace. He buried his face in her hair and didn't even seem to mind that it was hair the color of dead grass rather than ripening wheat.

Nola's mother was practically bouncing with joy. "Oh, your father is *so* pleased," she said. "And so's Grandmama, and the abbot, and Mother Superior—the baby, of course, is too young to understand—but King Fenuku is very excited. Whew!" She waved her hand in front of her nose.

As her mother continued to chatter, Nola shook her head. "I'm sorry," she told Galvin. "She gets these strange fancies—"

"Another never," Galvin told her. "*Never* apologize for your family."

Nola looked at her mother, looked back at Galvin, took a deep breath, and gave an emphatic nod. "You're right."

"Of course I am," Galvin said. He, too, took a deep breath. "And with that in mind," he told her, "you're going to *love* my mother."